THE LORD OF THE HIGHLANDS

BY PETER WACHT

Kestrel
Media Group, LLC

BOOK 5 OF THE SYLVAN CHRONICLES

Copyright 2020 © by Peter Wacht

Book design by ebooklaunch.com

Published in the United States by Kestrel Media Group LLC.

Kestrel
Media Group, LLC

ISBN: 978-1-950236-08-4
eBook ISBN: 978-1-950236-09-1

Library of Congress Control Number: 2020900164

ALSO BY PETER WACHT

THE SYLVAN CHRONICLES

The Legend of the Kestrel

The Call of the Sylvana

The Raptor of the Highlands

The Makings of a Warrior

The Lord of the Highlands

The Lost Kestrel Found (forthcoming)

The Claiming of the Highlands (forthcoming)

The Fight Against the Dark (forthcoming)

The Defender of the Light (forthcoming)

CHAPTER ONE

SOON TO HUNT

The raptor flew low over the trees, its long tail feathers barely missing the topmost branches. The bird of prey welcomed the rush of speed as its powerful wings brought it closer to the monstrous monolith that dominated the lush, green valley. The massive stone reared up before the magnificent bird. Tilting its wings, the raptor drifted to the left, catching an upward draft so that it could negotiate its way to the top.

As it circled the black, sheer stone, the raptor gradually gained altitude. The orange feathers lining its back glinted brightly as they caught the sun's rays, in contrast to the black and brown feathers that absorbed the light's energy. The heat from the sun energized the bird, building on the urgency it already felt. The raptor had seen much on its long journey through Fal Carrach, the kingdom that sat below the Highlands, as it watched from high above the earth.

Raptors were solitary creatures, defending a specific territory. That territory often stretched for dozens of leagues in every direction, limiting the contact between these ferocious birds of prey. A meeting of raptors was even rarer because they were so few in number. Nobles and other fortune seekers had hunted them almost to extinction during the last hundred years, hoping to turn a profit with the carcass of these legendary animals.

Strangely, since entering the Highlands from the south and finally reaching the Valley of the Crag, it had met three raptors. Yet, it was something else that made the creature wonder if the world was changing.

Reaching the top of the promontory, the raptor looked down on what had once been the mighty fortress of a mighty people. Selecting the highest vantage point, the bird settled onto the crumbling stone of one of the collapsed towers of the keep, its razor-sharp claws holding it steady as the strong winds of the Highlands tried to unseat it.

Meeting three of its kind in so short a span was unique, but that in itself wasn't enough to make the raptor look at the world differently. No, it was what the bird had observed in the south, something it had never expected to see. It was still early, perhaps too early to tell for sure if the sense of urgency the raptor felt building within it was justified. The great bird sensed a shift in nature itself, and that shift was beginning here – at the Crag.

Less than a decade before, the Crag had served as the capital of the Highlands — and home to the Marchers. Reputedly the best fighters in all the Kingdoms, as with any warrior, even the Marchers had a weakness. The Highlands was a rugged and dangerous land, and the same could be said of the Marchers, but, like the raptors, they were few in number.

When the betrayal occurred almost ten years before, though the Marchers fought valiantly, they could not prevent the inevitable. A once mighty fortress fell, and a once mighty people were defeated. Since that time, the plateau atop the monolith had lain abandoned. Moss had sprouted between the stones and the forest began its quest to reclaim its stolen territory.

The raptor shifted its right claw, adjusting for the wind. That tiny movement knocked away a small piece of moss, revealing the black stone beneath. Here, atop the Crag, the raptor felt the shift in nature even more, conscious of its growing strength and purpose. It sensed a new beginning. Hot blood was beginning to flow once more in the Highlands, beginning to stir, perhaps even boil, but only time would tell.

For it was still early. But it was still a beginning. The Highlands was again showing signs of life after ten years of treachery and oppression. And much like nature itself, the people of the Highlands were an unforgiving lot. For centuries, it had been said that like a raptor, to risk the wrath of a Marcher was to risk death – or worse.

As the raptor studied the harsh landscape of the Highlands, the sun began its slow descent in the west. Soon it would hunt, taking advantage of the dim light for an easy meal, for no creature could withstand the fury of a raptor's attack as the large bird hurtled down from the sky with breathtaking speed, its powerful wings drawn in, its sharp claws extended for its prey, the bird no more than a grey shadow in the sky. Much like the attack of a Marcher.

CHAPTER TWO

THE FEAST

"You still don't know if he has been freed?" Gregory whispered, not wanting Kaylie to overhear.

"No, milord," answered Kael, the Swordmaster bending down to keep his words discreet. "I haven't been able to find out a thing. None of the soldiers or servants are talking."

In any palace, the servants usually knew more of what was going on than anyone else. Keeping a secret in such a place was almost impossible. Yet this one had been kept, acknowledged Kael, and that's what worried him.

"It bothers me, milord."

"Me as well," said Gregory, who gave Sarelle a meaningful look.

The Queen of Benewyn sat next to Gregory at the head table in the main dining hall of the Palace, and on his other side sat Kaylie. They looked out on the dozens of tables below them filled with revelers. The Eastern Festival was coming to a close with a banquet to celebrate the contests won, the goods sold and the agreements made for the coming year.

"I think Rodric is up to something," said Sarelle.

She wore a dark green dress that set off her auburn hair perfectly. When Gregory had come to escort her to the banquet, upon seeing her he had become distinctly uncomfortable, just as Sarelle had desired. Yet her thoughts turned from romantic conquests to other things when Kael appeared. His report worried her as well. Something stirred in the Palace, and it wasn't for the good.

"I agree," said Gregory. "We should have had word of the boy's leaving by now."

"Agreed, milord." Kael, too, had gotten a bad feeling about this evening. "I've already alerted the men. We're packed and ready to go whenever you give the command."

Kael turned to Sarelle. "I've instructed Captain Fornier to do the same, Queen Sarelle. I hope that was not presumptuous of me."

"No, not at all," she replied, thankful that he had thought to prepare the captain of her guard. "I hope the good captain did not put up much of a fuss."

"He didn't, Queen Sarelle. He sensed it too and had already begun his own preparations. I've asked him to wait at the stables just in case the need arises. The men of Fal Carrach wait nearby."

Gregory smiled briefly. Leave it to Kael to think of everything. There had been no outward signs of trouble, yet little things had pricked at Gregory's sense of danger since the Trial. A few extra guards here, a few extra guards there. Restrictions on leaving the Palace. Subdued and quiet servants.

"Thank you, Kael. You've done well, as always."

"I simply do as you command, milord."

Kael stepped down from the dais and made his way out of the hall, wanting to sniff around for more clues. Gregory watched him go, thankful once again that Kael Bellilil had accepted his offer of employment so many years before.

"A good man there," said Sarelle.

"The best," answered Gregory.

He glanced to his right, checking on his daughter. It didn't appear as if she had heard anything. Good. He didn't want her to start worrying again.

Kaylie took no notice of the brief conversation held between her father, Sarelle and Kael. Her thoughts were elsewhere. When Thomas defeated the Makreen, a huge weight had been lifted from her chest. She hoped that he was back in the forest by now, and as far away from Tinnakilly as possible. Her eyes wandered over the hall several times, yet always came back to the young woman sitting a few seats to the right of the High King.

Corelia. She had shown far too much interest in Thomas after his victory. Far too much. Kaylie eyed the Princess of Armagh with suspicion. Corelia did nothing without good reason. As her eyes drifted down the head table, she locked gazes with Ragin for a brief moment, who gave her a leer that set her face afire. She tore her eyes away from him. Ragin had absolutely no shame. She was a fool for even being attracted to him at one time.

She was about to ask her father what he had been saying to Kael when she realized that conversation had died down within hall, the loud rumble of many voices talking and laughing replaced by almost total silence.

Looking toward the front of the hall, she gasped in shock. Her father jumped up from his chair, knocking it backward in his haste, his face red with anger.

"What is the meaning of this, Rodric?" he demanded. "The boy passed the Trial. He was to be set free!"

Thomas stood in the doorway, his legs and wrists chained. Two very large Dunmoorian soldiers dragged him into the banquet hall and past the startled revelers until he stood in front of the head table. Thomas appeared tired, yet defiant. His body was covered in bruises and dried blood, and no one had tended to his two wounds — the one on his forehead, the other on his side.

"True, Gregory," said Rodric, sitting comfortably in his chair as if nothing was amiss. "But it was not to be so. It seems the boy cannot suppress his true nature. Soon after he defeated the Makreen, we attempted to clean his wounds before letting him go. Throwing him out through the gates without any medical attention would have been inhumane."

The irony of what the High King had just said was not lost on those in the hall.

"Yet he would not allow us to help. The boy stabbed one physick with his own scalpel, nearly killing him. And he injured several of my men when they tried to bring him under control."

"And where is this physick?" asked Gregory. "And your injured men?"

Rodric was lying through his teeth, but Gregory could do nothing about it. His worst fear was becoming a reality and explained the tense atmosphere of the Palace. Rodric never had any intention of letting the boy go. That realization set his mind wondering once again as to why this boy was so important to him.

He remained standing, flexing his fists in an effort to control his temper. Rodric was flouting the laws of the Kingdoms with this charade, yet no one was in a position to stop him. This was not a good sign at all. He glanced quickly to the back of the hall and saw Kael standing by the door. The Highlander nodded. At least they were prepared. Now the question was, what could he do about this, if anything?

"In the infirmary, I'm afraid. Their severe injuries prevent them from being here."

Rodric had expected such a question from Gregory, knowing he would not be satisfied with his explanation. In fact, he had created his own casualties to complete the scheme if needed.

"It was truly an unfortunate episode, yet if you need proof, my son Ragin was there, and I'm sure he'd be willing to fill in all the details."

All eyes in the banquet hall turned to Ragin, who looked back rather smugly. He studied Thomas for a moment, pleased by his condition, before slowly rising from his chair.

CHAPTER THREE

ON THE TRAIL

"Two or three days old," said Catal Huyuk, rising from where he crouched in the grass.

"As I thought," grunted Rynlin, not really paying attention.

Rynlin had met Beluil in the clearing at the western edge of Oakwood Forest in the late morning. Luckily, Catal Huyuk was actually on the way to the Isle of Mist when he answered Rynlin's call for help, sensing his need through his necklace. Beluil waited impatiently at one side of the clearing, eager to continue the hunt.

"Thomas put up quite a fight," said the dangerous-looking man, the blades of his many weapons gleaming in the sun. As he walked around the glade, he replayed the skirmish through his mind. "He was heavily outnumbered, but killed four or five, maybe more. He must have fought like a demon." Pride was clear in his voice.

Rynlin continued to stare at a particular spot in the grass, his anger raging within him. As soon as he arrived in the clearing, he had searched the surrounding area thoroughly, looking for some clue as to what had

9

happened. Eventually, he came back to the blanket and basket of food — and the wine bottle. One sniff told him everything he needed to know. Once again someone had taken his grandson. His grandson! His only grandson!

"Let's get going," Rynlin said, coming out of his trance. "The Eastern Festival is coming to a close. There's only one place he could have been taken."

Catal Huyuk nodded, following after Rynlin and Beluil as they walked out onto the grasslands. Thomas was Rynlin's grandson, but for Catal Huyuk he was something more — hope for the future, a bright light to follow in the coming darkness. Whoever had taken Thomas had made a grave mistake.

CHAPTER FOUR

CHANGING WINDS

"Lords and ladies, it is— it is true."

Ragin's voice wavered. Gregory's open disbelief unnerved him a bit. Ragin scanned the back of the banquet hall, the dozens of Armaghian soldiers lining the walls renewing his confidence.

"The physick attempted to examine his wounds. We expected him to be tired, to be grateful for the attention, but no."

Ragin appeared saddened by what he was about to relate. "He grabbed a scalpel from the physick's bag and stabbed the good man in the gut. He then went after me and my men, several of whom were injured while subduing him. After a great deal of struggle, we finally stopped him from injuring anyone else. As the Prince of Armagh, I swear it as the truth."

Ragin immediately dropped back into his seat at a barely noticeable motion from his father. He had wanted to say more, perhaps embellish his role in the charade, but his father had told him exactly what to say — and to say only that. By the feverish look in his father's eyes, now was not the time to cross him.

Kaylie looked from her father to Rodric. The two were locked in a battle of wills. For the first time she saw a murderous glare on her father's face and knew for a fact that if Rodric stood any closer, the High King would be dead. Her anger matched her father's, that and her disbelief.

Ragin sworn as Prince of Armagh! The thought was ludicrous. Everyone knew him to be a liar, yet no one would challenge him. Not here anyway. Kaylie could see that her father had already considered such an action, but wisely chose not to. When Thomas entered the chamber, the soldiers of Dunmoor and Armagh silently had taken up positions along the back wall.

There was nothing she or her father could do. Gregory cursed in frustration, knowing full well that even though his men could defeat the soldiers of any other Kingdom, they were outnumbered here at the Palace. Even with the addition of Sarelle's troops, the skirmish would be a short one.

Gregory suddenly realized what he was considering. An uprising against the High King? In the middle of Dunmoor? Some might call it treason, others a necessity. Times had changed drastically in just a few days, and for the worse. Rodric was pushing against the fragile balance of power within the Kingdoms. If he continued, that balance would disintegrate.

"Obviously you have taken every precaution, Rodric. You have won this time, but this is only the first battle." Gregory sat back down in his chair, gripping the ornately carved wooden arms tightly.

The audience watched the entire episode in rapt attention, sensing that a change of some sort was taking place. What effect it would have was still in question, yet all knew it revolved around the boy standing before the head table — the boy in chains, his body covered in blood, bruises and cuts; the boy who had defeated the Makreen; the boy who should be free. Anyone with the tiniest bit of political sense knew that Rodric had orchestrated a sham, but like Gregory, they too saw the Armaghian and Dunmoorian soldiers standing behind them.

"Then justice will finally be done," said Rodric, motioning to a guard standing by the door, who immediately ran out into the hallway shouting orders.

Kaylie stared at Thomas with tears in her eyes. He was going to die, and it was all her fault. She could hear her father cursing softly next to her, Sarelle's hand covering his own to offer comfort, his voice rife with frustration at not being able to help the boy standing before them. The words tyranny, murder and false accusation mixed with greed and power as Gregory spouted an invective-filled tirade. She glanced quickly at Rodric. Next to him Ragin smiled with glee, clearly enjoying the spectacle unfolding before him.

Corelia, on the other hand, studied Thomas much like a predator before a kill. The look she gave him — calculating, shrewd, suggestive — made her skin crawl. There had to be something Kaylie could do. Anything. She leaned forward in her chair, her grief threatening to overwhelm her. It was hopeless. There was nothing for her to do but watch the one person who had treated her as a friend die because of her foolishness.

"We have a criminal before us," intoned Rodric, speaking as a judge would before an execution. "Justice will be done. Bring him here."

The two guards standing behind Thomas shoved him forward, knocking him to the ground because of the chains around his ankles.

"Perhaps the demonstration that follows will show that such crimes are not permitted in the Kingdoms, and that as High King, I will do whatever necessary to ensure my law is upheld."

Many of the lords and ladies turned shocked expressions to the High King, realizing the true meaning of his words. Rodric was going to punish the boy right here. More important, he had said *my law*. Not *the law*. Murmurs of discontent ran through the crowd, but quickly ceased when several Armaghian soldiers stepped forward. The winds of change blew strong and cold.

The soldier quickly returned, followed by a dozen more pushing a cart carrying a large piece of wood. It resembled something the hangman would use, in that the two large pieces of oak ran perpendicular to one another. At the end of the smaller piece another block of oak ran crosshairs to it. Attached to that piece were long black chains with manacles affixed to their ends.

The soldiers moved slowly toward the head table, grunting with effort as they approached. Everyone watched in horrified fascination as the soldiers set one end of the wood structure onto the bottom of the cart.

The two soldiers guarding Thomas then removed the manacles from his wrists and ankles, revealing the bloody skin rubbed raw by the steel, and placed the other manacles around his wrists. The soldiers then used rope tied to the top of the piece of wood to pull the structure upright, dragging Thomas backward until he was hoisted into the air. They then placed several steel pins at the foot of the wood block to keep it in position.

To Kaylie, it seemed as if Thomas had been placed on the gallows. The chains spread Thomas' arms wide, tearing open the wound in his side once more. A slow trickle of blood began to run down his leg, dripping from his foot onto the cart floorboards. Kaylie wanted to avert her eyes, as many of the ladies in the banquet hall had already done, unable to bear the condition Thomas was in. Instead, she forced herself to look at him.

As her eyes ran over his body, she saw the many scars running across his back and chest, the very sight of them making her sick to her stomach. Still, she refused to look away. During the past two days Thomas had demonstrated remarkable courage. She would try to do the same, little good that it would do.

"I see you are not a stranger to the whip," said Rodric. "Good. Then you are familiar with what is to happen next. I will save you from the pain if you will admit your guilt. Will you, boy? Will you admit your guilt?"

Rodric did not wait for a response, not really expecting, or even wanting, one. This lesson was only in part for Thomas. He motioned to a soldier standing by the hangman's block who held a barbed whip in his hand. He stepped behind Thomas, flicking the long, black leather behind his back before swinging forward violently. The whip dug deeply into Thomas' flesh, the sharp crack echoing in the silent chamber. The soldier drew the whip back again, and again, until each sharp crack drifted into the one preceding it.

Gregory felt sick to his stomach. Everyone in the hall knew what Rodric had planned for Thomas, yet still he had to go through with this act. This wasn't justice. This was revenge. This was a statement. And for what? Gregory promised himself that he would find out, and that he would pay back Rodric many times over for the pain he caused this innocent boy. Gregory's futility ate into his heart, filling it with despair. The boy had saved his life, and his daughter's life twice, and he could not return the favor.

Thomas kept his head lowered as the whip bit sharply into his flesh. He was beyond pain now. His waning energy decreased with each strike of the barbed leather. He wanted only to escape the pain now, having lost the desire to fight. He had driven his body too far. Now he just wanted to rest, to let go. The struggle had become too much to bear.

CHAPTER FIVE

DEFIANCE

"A fool hangs before us," said Rodric, laughing softly. "Admit your guilt, boy!"

Rodric's taunting words streaked through the cool, inviting blackness that slowly enveloped Thomas, striking a chord within him. He had never given in to anything before, not without a fight, and he was not about to do so now. Not to Rodric of all people.

Calling upon what little strength remained, Thomas struggled to lift his head, the simple movement feeling like the hardest thing he had ever had to do. Finally he stared straight ahead, his eyes smoldering with green fire as he glowered defiantly at the High King.

Rodric matched his gaze briefly, but could not bear it for long. He cursed himself for a coward, telling himself not to give in to the boy. But he couldn't hold that gaze. No matter. The boy wouldn't be around for much longer.

"Let everyone see what happens to those who challenge the power of the High King," he muttered angrily. He motioned for the soldier to continue.

The whip bit into Thomas with a renewed vigor, yet he barely felt it. Strangely, a small smile crept onto Thomas' face. Even now, Rodric was a coward.

Gregory watched the entire episode, appalled by what was happening. As his eyes wandered around the room, he saw much the same expression on other faces — shock and dawning recognition. This spectacle was as much for the boy as for them, they realized. Rodric was demonstrating his power, and what would happen to any who got in his way. The winds of change blew stronger, howling of what was to come. Gregory sensed that a dark winter was almost upon them.

His anger grew hotter and hotter until it burned brightly within him. Gregory's hand rubbed the hilt of his dagger. He had to stop this. Rodric could not be allowed to carry on in this way. He began pushing himself up from his chair, his eyes staring intently at the High King, when a strong hand on his shoulder forced him back down.

Infuriated, Gregory whipped around. Kael stood behind him, his hand now resting comfortably on his shoulder. Kael shook his head slightly. Gregory reluctantly acknowledged the truth of his current dilemma. Acting now would be suicide. He took a few deep breaths and made himself relax.

Kael had seen Gregory's intentions in his posture, having served with the King of Fal Carrach long enough to know his habits. Gregory had considered killing the High King right there, and though a worthy idea, it would have done them little good.

He probably would have succeeded, but the boy would have died anyway, as would Gregory, Sarelle and all of their men. They were outnumbered ten to one in the Palace by the Dunmoorian and Armaghian troops. If Rodric openly murdered the boy, why not two sovereigns as well? No, now was not the time to act. Later, when the odds were more in their favor.

Kael tried to turn a dispassionate eye to the whipping, having seen many horrible things during his life as a soldier. The boy continued to stare straight ahead, his green eyes burning with anger. Judging by the marks already on the boy's body, his life had been hard. Still, his ability to deal with the pain was remarkable. As he studied the boy's features, there was a certain familiarity about him.

He looked very much like a Highlander, though not completely. Perhaps just his mother or father. There was a strength in him not seen in most. A pity that it would be wasted, stolen from him by a vindictive bastard. The boy did not deserve to die, but again, there was nothing he could do. At the moment anyway. But on another day perhaps he would be in a position to pay back the High King. It was the least he could do for his countryman.

As the whip cracked against Thomas' back, every muscle in his body quivered in protest. He tried desperately to hold back the pain, but it became harder and harder with each stroke. His strength continued to drain away, and with it his desire. He was tired. Tired of the pain, the struggle.

The blackness that had welcomed him in the cell beneath the Palace had returned, beckoning to him, caressing him. If he would just let go, he would find the peace he sought, away from the pain, free from the struggle. The blackness was so inviting. Thomas reached out for it, letting it soothe his weariness, his pain—

No! He couldn't allow it. Not yet. Thomas drew away from the darkness, running from it. Inviting it may be, but once he gave in to it, he'd never escape. No! He refused to give Rodric the satisfaction. He would never surrender. Never! Talyn Kestrel would look on him with shame if he did. If he was to die this day, then so be it. He would die with honor just like his grandfather did those many years before.

Thomas held his head up, eyes burning brightly. He may not be able to escape the situation, but he would meet whatever came next with dignity. If nothing else, when his grandparents heard what had happened to him, at least they could be proud of him. There was nothing left to him but that now. Nothing at all. His hope for survival had been quashed as soon as he saw Chertney sitting behind the High King.

"You call this justice, Rodric?" Gregory asked angrily. The whipping stopped as Gregory spoke. "This is torture. End this demonstration, Rodric. We all know who it is really meant for."

"I don't know what you mean, Gregory."

Rodric turned toward the King of Fal Carrach, his voice filled with poison and hate. He was clearly enjoying himself, and he would decide when it came to an end.

"This boy is a criminal, and according to the law criminals are punished."

"Don't hide behind the law, Rodric. The boy doesn't deserve this. No one does."

"On the contrary," said Rodric, almost spitting out the words, "He does!" Rodric motioned to one of his captains, who waited patiently by the door.

Gregory cursed himself for a fool. His mind worked furiously, once again looking for a way to put a stop to this horrific spectacle. Yet he could think of nothing. And at the same time he put himself and his daughter in greater danger. He looked at Sarelle, hoping she might have a solution to their dilemma.

She shrugged her shoulders apologetically, the sympathy in her eyes plain. The captain Rodric had motioned to led a squad of soldiers to where Gregory, Kaylie and Sarelle sat. Rodric held all the cards at the moment. Gregory wondered just how far Rodric would go.

The whipping continued, the soldier's motion slow and methodical. Kaylie couldn't bear to watch any longer. How could she have done such a horrible thing? How could she? Every time the whip struck Thomas' body, she winced. Tears streamed down her face. Because of her Thomas was going to die. She buried her head in her hands, hearing an accusation with each crack of the whip: *Traitor. Murderer. Traitor. Murderer.* She jumped when she felt a gentle touch on her forearm.

"Watch this, Kaylie," said her father softly, but his eyes intent. "I know this is difficult, but you must learn from it. See the people we are dealing with for what they truly are. Give Thomas the respect and honor he has earned." Raising her head and wiping away her tears, she forced herself to watch.

"Enough," said Rodric, an evil grin on his face. The hall was silent. Thomas turned his head back toward Rodric, forcing the High King to look away. "My man's arm is tired. We will soften the boy up a bit before we continue. Place him closer to the fire."

Rodric's squad of soldiers hastened forward to obey, pushing the cart as close to the fireplace as they could without having to worry about it catching fire. A rumble of conversation started up in the hall then, with many averting their eyes. Rodric had gone too far. This lesson was becoming more terrible by the second.

As the soldiers added wood to the fire, the flames licked higher and higher until they almost touched the soles of Thomas' feet. Two soldiers stood guard, one on each side, but they served little purpose. There was no place Thomas could go, and the finality of his situation began to set in.

Most of the people in the hall could no longer bear to look at him or at Rodric. The High King was enjoying himself immensely, laughing heartily and joking with Loris and Ragin, the black shadow of Chertney hovering behind them. To see humor in such a situation was sickening. Thomas looked around the room, taking it all in. No one could help him now. No one. His head slumped against his chest, the pain and heat both working against him now.

CHAPTER SIX

FINDING HIS WAY

V oices began to whisper through Thomas' mind, their words drifting in and out of his consciousness. *Let go. Let go. Welcome the peace.* He fought against them, trying to open his eyes, but found the effort to be too much. *Let your burdens go. Let them go.*

Maybe he should. No, he had to remain strong. He had to. He had sworn an oath to his grandfather. He had promised to free the Highlands. *But the Highlanders never cared about you.* The voices were right. They thought he was a strange little boy, the son of a witch. *Why should you care about them? Why?*

Light dances with dark, green fire burns in the night, hopes and dreams follow the wind, to fall in black and white. The prophecy. Rynlin had told him he was the one. He was to become the Defender of the Light. And Thomas knew it was true. He had discovered that much after joining the Sylvana. He couldn't give in now. There was too much he had to do. Too much that was required of him, whether he wanted it or not.

Let go. Let go. The voices continued to play through his mind and he struggled to ignore them, the battle raging within him for several seconds. He fought to open his eyes, and after what seemed like an eternity, he finally succeeded. He felt the silver of his necklace, given to him by his grandfather in memory of his mother, the same necklace that confirmed his place among the Sylvana, on his skin. The necklace that had guided him to safety from under the Crag.

The voices receded into the darkness, watching, waiting, knowing that soon their time would come. Soon Thomas would be too weak to stop their inevitable whisperings. Thomas tried to concentrate, using the necklace as his focal point. He had to find a way to escape. There was too much depending on him. But how? There had to be a way. At the very least he had to try.

The heat of the flames licked the soles of his feet, and instinctively he raised them. One of the guards at his side roughly knocked them back down with the haft of his spear. Maybe there was a way he could escape, if he still had the strength. His grandparents had always said he was as loud as an elephant when using the Talent. In fact, he had even seen an elephant once not too long ago, when Rynlin took him on a trip—

Thomas forced his mind back to its purpose. He had to concentrate, otherwise he was going to die. Thomas freed some of the pain he had locked away in the back of his mind. His back immediately sizzled and his side ached. The pain burned away the blackness, allowing for a clarity of thought that had escaped Thomas for most of the last two days.

Thomas reached for the Talent. He was able to grab it with his fingernails, his hold tenuous. Gradually, he pulled more of the power in, allowing it to wash through his body, giving him renewed energy and cleansing his wounds. He reveled in the strength it gave him.

Delicately he mixed its power with that created by the fire beneath him. He glanced quickly at Chertney to see if he had noticed, but the shadowy warlock had not, the energy of the fire masking his work. Chertney was deep in conversation with Rodric, who scowled at much of what he had to say. Good, very good. Thomas knew he was in no condition to challenge the warlock, so he would have to be extremely careful.

Slowly, Thomas pulled himself up, taking hold of the chains with his hands just above the manacles around his wrists. He then channeled a tiny bit of the Talent into the manacles. The Talent was completely undetectable, as the heat of the fire hid it from Chertney, who continued to lecture Rodric. In just a few seconds, the links of chain connected to the manacles melted.

He was free! He forced himself to remain calm. There was still much to do, but at least the first part of his plan had succeeded. He looked around quickly, pleased to see that no one had taken notice of what he had done. No one wanted to see what he endured.

Continuing to hold onto the chains, he surveyed the banquet hall, looking for a way to escape. The possibility of surviving rejuvenated him a bit, but his weakness remained despite the help of the Talent. Whatever he was going to do, he had to do it soon.

There, just above him. A banner hung down from the ceiling. He could climb that to the unoccupied balcony. Yes, that was certainly a possibility. But would he be able to pull himself up the twenty feet of cloth to make it there? Maybe, maybe not. Nothing else came to mind. He was about to make his move when a voice cut through the din.

"Bring him forward," shouted Rodric. "It is time to administer the sentence."

Chertney sat smugly next to the High King, obviously pleased that he had gotten his way. In his opinion, it was time to put an end to this ridiculousness and to remove this threat. The squad of soldiers pushed the cart forward again, struggling somewhat with the weight, as Thomas' two guards followed along.

Thomas had to think quickly. His primary escape route had just vanished. He knew what was coming next, so he had to move now. He looked around the room desperately. Finally, something came to him. It was a gamble, but it was all he had left.

The cart stopped a few feet in front of Rodric, and the squad of soldiers returned to their positions along the walls. Rodric pulled his sword free of its sheath, running his hand along the edge of the blade, testing its sharpness. Satisfied, he turned his attention back to Thomas.

"It has been fun, boy, but all good things must come to an end." Rodric crossed his arms, resting the blade on his shoulder. "Unfortunately, now it is time for you to leave us. Will you admit your crimes?"

Much to everyone's surprise, the stoic warrior responded. "You are a coward, Rodric. Next time we meet, it will be you who feels the pain."

Thomas' words were soft, but everyone in the banquet hall heard them. Several people gasped at his daring. Then again, he didn't have anything to lose.

Rodric laughed harshly, if only to cover his growing fear. Thomas' sharp green eyes and the certainty of his words frightened him. Rodric was not a very good king, but he was a very good actor.

"Brave words, boy. But we will not be meeting again. Guards!"

Two guards entered the room carrying a large chopping block. The banquet hall became deathly silent, as all eyes turned toward the grim procession. Thomas realized that now was the time to act. Kicking out with his foot, he caught one of his guards squarely in the face. The soldier dropped his spear, sprawling on the floor. Thomas released the chains and dropped to the ground. He had a hard time maintaining his balance, but miraculously he remained on his feet, the adrenaline rushing through his body giving him a newfound strength.

Grabbing the spear on the ground, he ducked under the jab of the other soldier, then pushed his own spear deep into his gut. The soldier collapsed, shrieking in pain, blood pouring out onto the stone. Thomas pulled his spear free then stabbed the other soldier in the back as he tried to regain his feet. Now was not the time to fight honorably. Now was the time to fight for survival.

Bedlam immediately broke out in the banquet hall as Rodric's soldiers rushed forward, trying to push their way through the crowd of lords and ladies, who in turn were trying to exit the banquet hall. Another soldier charged toward Thomas, his sword raised above his head. Thomas caught hold of the man's wrist as he brought the blade down and flipped him over his back, at the same time wrenching the blade from his hand. He dispatched him with a slash to the chest. Thomas leapt over the head table going right past Chertney, who was too surprised to react, and slipped through the doorway partially hidden by a large tapestry.

Rodric issued orders in a rage at the embarrassment of having his prisoner escape so easily. Screaming for more guards, he ordered the gates closed, then stormed after Thomas with his men in tow.

As he watched the High King leave, Gregory sat there calmly at first, but could contain himself for only a short time. Deep laughter escaped from him, the image of the enraged High King dancing in front of his eyes. Kael laughed as well, he too having seen the humor in the situation.

"That boy is more than he seems," Gregory whispered to himself.

Rising from his chair, he motioned to Sarelle and Kaylie. They were leaving. Kael took the lead as they pushed their way through the crowd toward the stables.

CHAPTER SEVEN

DESPERATE GAMBLE

Thomas dashed through the opening, the commotion behind him driving him forward despite his weariness. Sword at the ready, he ran through Loris' private study and yanked open the door on the other side. Two guards stood there, not expecting someone other than the King of Dunmoor to exit the room.

Thomas swept by them before they could react, slashing one soldier's hamstring, then slicing across the other's knee. Both collapsed to the floor in agony, their legs useless. He headed for the nearest staircase and went down, hoping to escape the fortress before the search could be organized.

He was certain that if he could get back into the dungeon he could escape through one of the secret passages he had sensed the night before. Once he got underneath the Palace, his pursuers would be at a disadvantage. Then he'd be free of the keep with none the wiser.

Thomas moved quietly down the shadowy hallways and staircases, eyes sweeping from side to side to make sure he was alone. He was almost to the dungeon when he was forced to stop. He leaned back against the wall where several hallways met, trying to push himself into it. A troop of Dunmoorian soldiers charged down an adjacent hallway and through the crossing. Thomas waited breathlessly as they passed, thankful that none had thought to look closely in his direction.

Poking his head around the corner he cursed his bad luck. He was too slow! A dozen soldiers waited at the other end of the hallway that led to the dungeon. His options were disappearing quickly, and with it his chances for escape. Once all the exits on the lower floors of the Palace had been sealed, roving groups of soldiers would move steadily upward, eventually sniffing him out.

Thomas frantically scanned the surrounding area for another way out. Nothing. He made a quick decision. They wanted him to go up, he'd go up. He'd just go faster than they expected.

Thomas ran back the way he had come, heading for the upper levels. He was almost to the staircase when he burst into a group of soldiers coming the other way and ended up face to face with Kaylie. Caught unawares by his arrival, the soldiers quickly recovered upon seeing his sword, hands reaching for their blades. Out of options, Thomas grabbed Kaylie and pulled her close, placing his blade against her neck. She gasped in fear as the cold metal caressed her throat. The horrible feeling that she was about to get what she deserved flashed through her mind.

"Keep you swords sheathed," warned Thomas, his voice quiet and calm, though his eyes burned fiercely.

Kael gave a short signal with his hand and the soldiers relaxed their grips.

A bolt of fear shot through Gregory at seeing his daughter in danger. "Thomas, please let her go," he said, seeing how close to the edge Thomas really was. Who could blame him? He was a hunted man with no way out, other than death. "I promise we won't try to stop you. I promise."

Thomas stared at Gregory for several long seconds, seeing the paralyzing worry cross the older man's face. Abruptly he pulled his sword away and pushed Kaylie back toward her father.

"I would never hurt her, even now."

Gregory hugged Kaylie close to him, relief flooding through him. "I know," he said softly. "I know."

Thomas turned away from father and daughter, making his way through the soldiers toward the staircase. They stepped out of his way, several nodding their heads in respect. Some had seen what he had done in the pit, and then what he had endured in the banquet hall. Others had heard from their comrades. Many wanted to help him escape, but knew they couldn't under the current circumstances. They saw in Thomas what they saw in themselves — a soldier, and a man of honor.

"Thomas," Kaylie called quietly, stepping away from her father.

A lump formed in her throat as he turned his sharp eyes on her. There was so much she wanted to say, but she didn't know where to begin.

"I'm sorry. I'm truly sorry. I didn't know this was going to happen."

As Thomas looked at Kaylie, his eyes softened for a moment, then hardened once again. He nodded sharply then bolted up the stairs. Kaylie stared after him until her father gently took her arm and led her in the other direction. There was so much more she wanted to say. So much more. And now she'd probably never get the chance.

Chapter Eight

Cornered

G regory and his party had almost reached the stables when Rodric and Chertney appeared before them, a large group of soldiers at their backs. Kael and Captain Fornier, a rugged man with a short, pointy beard, placed themselves in front of Gregory and Sarelle.

"Leaving, Gregory?" Rodric stood akimbo, his voice confident, though his eyes were less so. His plans had been torn apart, and he was trying frantically to put them back together.

"Yes, we are," replied Gregory, his voice cold.

"I can't allow it."

"You can't allow—"

"The boy will be cornered in minutes," said Rodric, cutting Gregory off. "Then his sentence will be carried out. Once that has been accomplished, you may go, of course. But not before. We will need unbiased witnesses for the execution."

Rodric smiled disingenuously, while Chertney stood glaring at Rodric. The shadowy figure obviously was less than pleased by what had happened.

There was something about Chertney that bothered Gregory, but now was not the time to think on it. Though he had wanted to wipe that smug expression from Rodric's face, he knew his decision had already been made for him. He and his men were obviously outnumbered, and he couldn't put his daughter and Sarelle in danger just because he itched for a fight. Besides, such an action on his part would not help the boy escape. Thomas, he corrected himself. Calling him a boy now was an insult.

"As you say," said Gregory, clearly not liking the taste of his words, but having no other choice.

"Good," said Rodric, clapping his hands with pleasure. Events were finally moving the way he wanted again.

Rodric and Chertney joined Gregory and his soldiers quickly circled the group. When Sarelle gave Rodric a questioning glance, he simply mumbled something about an honor guard before directing them back the way they had come, toward the staircases leading to the upper floors of the Palace. They knew the truth, however, and honor had nothing to do with it.

Kaylie marched along quietly, her thoughts on Thomas. She continued to flay herself mentally for her stupidity. Lost in her thoughts, she didn't realize who walked next to her.

"An intriguing creature, this Thomas, is he not?"

Corelia almost purred as the question escaped her lips. Her eyes danced with pleasure as she considered the boy who was causing so much trouble for her father.

"Excuse me?" asked Kaylie, clearly not pleased that she was stuck next to the Princess of Armagh as she climbed the many flights of stairs.

"Thomas. He seems to be full of surprises."

"Yes, he seems to be," she answered noncommittally, not wanting to discuss him with the likes of her.

"I'm told you were his friend for a time."

Kaylie flinched as if she had been physically struck. She had been his friend, but no more.

"What is he like?" Corelia waited hungrily for her response. To Kaylie she resembled a predator circling for the kill.

"I'm sorry, but I really don't know him very well." She hoped that would put an end to the conversation.

Corelia knew that Kaylie held something back, but decided to let it drop. She couldn't resist a final dig, however.

"A pity, then, to have wasted your time with him." Corelia smiled innocently, though the look she gave Kaylie spoke volumes. "He seems to have many talents indeed."

Kaylie stared at the tall blond with daggers in her eyes. She thought of several biting responses, but did not have the time to voice them. They had reached the battlements. In her heart, she knew the drama of the past day was about to come to an end.

CHAPTER NINE

FINAL STEP

T homas ran steadily upward, intent on making his way to the battlements. He paid almost no attention to the soldiers who appeared before him. To him, they were simply obstacles in his path. His actions were based on theirs. Several soldiers had no desire to fight him one on one, knowing that he had defeated the Makreen, and wisely stepped out of the way.

Others made the mistake of challenging him. Thomas let his instincts take over then, his thoughts focused on his goal. When he finally reached the top, he couldn't remember how many soldiers he had killed or injured along the way, and he didn't really care. Only one thing mattered now — survival — and he would do whatever was necessary to ensure it.

The battlements of the Palace were simple in design, which showed the age of the fortress. Creativity was not a consideration when castles like this one had been built. Security was the first concern, practicality the second, thus four turrets stood on each end of the Palace, and a fifth rose above them in the very center of the keep.

Thomas ran to the wall and poked his head through the crenels. The Palace was built on a high slope above the town of Tinnakilly, and the eastern wall, on which Thomas currently stood, looked out over The Gullet — the waterway that connected Stormy Bay to the Inland Sea. The fortress wall dropped several hundred feet to the rocks below, now getting pounded by the rising evening tide.

Thomas grabbed the gritty surface of one of the crenels and was about to pull himself up when several familiar clicks stopped him. They had found him. He turned around slowly. Soldiers poured onto the battlements, forming a large semicircle around him. In front of them stood several soldiers, the familiar click signifying that their crossbow bolts were loaded and ready to shoot.

Above the soldiers, on the central turret, Rodric and Chertney appeared, and next to them Gregory, Sarelle and Kaylie, none of whom looked very happy at being there. Thomas clenched his hands in frustration. He had gotten so close. It couldn't end like this?

"Once again you have done a remarkable job of preserving your life, but no more," pronounced Rodric, his voice carrying on the wind over the entire battlements. "Kill him."

Thomas crouched and balanced on the balls of his feet, assuming a warrior's stance taught to him by Antonin, one that the legendary warrior had used to defeat supposedly insurmountable odds. The crossbowmen's' fingers tightened on their triggers at the High King's command, but another voice forced them to relax their grips.

"Hold," shouted Ragin, pushing his way through the soldiers' ranks to stand before the archers.

Thomas looked at Ragin with a quizzical expression. He had absolutely no idea what was going on.

Ragin turned toward his father. "Milord, I captured this scoundrel," he said loudly. "I request permission to carry out the sentence."

Ragin's plan had formed in his mind during Thomas' attempted escape. The boy was dangerous, that was true. But he was also injured and had lost a lot of blood.

As he saw it, since Thomas was tired and weak, there would be no better opportunity for Ragin to challenge him, when the risk of doing so was minimal. By killing the bastard in a fair fight, he would raise his stature considerably, especially since Thomas had killed the Makreen. In time, Ragin would become a legend as the story passed from one mouth to the next.

The same thoughts passed through Rodric's mind as he pondered the situation he had been boxed into by his son. He suddenly realized that either his son was smarter than he thought, or considerably dumber. True, now was the best time to defeat the boy. Then again, Thomas had proven remarkably resilient and dangerous.

He doubted his son had considered the fact that a cornered animal was the fiercest of all. Probably not. His son's vision was most likely clouded by his dreams of glory. But Rodric could think of no way to stop him without making Ragin appear weak. Then, by association, others would perceive Rodric as weak. That was something he couldn't allow.

"Fool," muttered Kael, in reference to Ragin.

Gregory nodded his agreement. Maybe something good would come from this after all, he thought cold-bloodedly.

"So be it," answered Rodric. His son was on his own.

The crossbowmen immediately lowered their weapons and backed away from Ragin, giving him room to maneuver. Thomas smiled as the Prince of Armagh approached him with his sword drawn. Perhaps he could escape after all, with Ragin's unknowing assistance.

"You were lucky against the Makreen," said Ragin, loud enough for the soldiers behind him to hear. "But luck will not be enough against me."

Ragin charged forward, swinging his blade at Thomas' head in a killing blow. Thomas deflected the attack with his sword and tried to dart away, but found that he couldn't. He was too tired, too weak, and, as a result, too slow. The Prince of Armagh continued to pound away at his defenses as Thomas remained backed against the outer stone curtain. Ragin was rested and prepared to fight. All Thomas could do was parry the thrusts and chops directed at him. He quickly concluded that if he didn't do something soon, he was going to die.

With some effort, Thomas parried Ragin's next slash and counterattacked, swinging low, then high, hoping to catch his opponent off guard. He succeeded, his blade cutting deeply into Ragin's left arm. The Prince of Armagh scurried back, yelling more in shock than pain. Ragin looked down at his arm in anger, the blood staining his shirt a dark red. Growling in fury, he charged forward again, reason now replaced by emotion.

Thomas calmly stood there waiting for him. Ragin might be good with a blade, but he didn't have the slightest grasp of strategy. With one stroke, Thomas had seized control of the duel. Catching Ragin's blade on his own, Thomas slammed his shoulder into the Prince of Armagh, knocking him against the battlements. Before he could recover, Thomas slashed at Ragin, catching him across the face.

Ragin screamed in pain as the blade sliced through his right eye. Dropping his sword and falling to the ground, Ragin writhed on the stone battlements in agony, his bloody hands covering his ravaged face. Thomas considered finishing the job, then thought better of it. Everyone else on the battlements was so surprised by what had happened that none of the soldiers had reacted yet. Now was his chance.

Pulling himself up onto one of the crenels, Thomas looked down at the pounding surf below. It was now or never. Turning back toward the High King, Thomas grabbed the hilt of his sword with two hands and brought it behind his head. With the last of his strength, he threw it toward the High King.

"Kill him!" shouted Rodric, his wits finally returning.

The High King no longer paid attention to Thomas, horror consuming him at his son's fate. Chertney quickly stepped forward, using his Black Magic to divert the blade, which would have flown true otherwise. A pity really, thought Chertney. He probably should have let the boy's blade strike home. Then one problem would have been eliminated. Ah, well. He would just have to wait a little longer.

The soldiers on the battlements were released from their stupor by Rodric's shout, raising their crossbows and releasing their bolts in a single motion. Thomas caught the movement from the corner of his eye. Spinning around he took a deep breath and jumped off the battlements. The bolts passed through the air where he had been just a second before.

"Thomas!" Kaylie screamed, as he disappeared from view.

She threw herself into her father's arms, sobbing uncontrollably. Her one true friend was dead, all because of her.

Gregory motioned to Kael, who immediately formed up his men. They were leaving. Right now. No one bothered to stop the grim-faced men as they made for the staircase leading down toward the stables.

The Armaghian soldiers ran toward the battlements and looked down at the water pounding against the rocks. "No one could have survived that," said one. Several nodded in agreement. They didn't notice that Chertney had joined them. When they did, they immediately backed away.

"Even so," the dark shadow of a man said ominously, "find his body and bring it to me."

The soldiers immediately ran off to obey, not wanting to spend any more time in his presence than necessary. Chertney examined the rocks below for some time. He was beginning to think he might have misjudged this boy. Chertney hoped, for his own sake, that was not the case. Otherwise, a very unpleasant task awaited him.

CHAPTER TEN

FREEDOM

Thomas opened himself to the Talent as soon as he jumped off the battlements, the familiar feeling giving him some comfort as he plummeted toward the rocks below. He needed to act quickly or all his efforts would be wasted.

He formed the image of the raptor in his mind and began the difficult process of guiding the power of nature into the form.

He wasn't going to make it. He wasn't strong enough to control the tremendous power needed to succeed.

The rocks came up too fast. Pushing thoughts of failure from his mind, Thomas searched within himself for some hidden reserve of energy. There had to be something left. There had to be!

As the rocks rose up to meet him, he felt the Talent finally take hold. Thomas squawked in victory as he transformed himself into the raptor, his wings catching the winds as he soared over the rocks with just a few feet to spare.

He flew to the east, hoping that his strength would last long enough for him to reach safety. Even now, as he allowed the breezes to push him across The Gullet, he felt the last of his energy slipping away.

CHAPTER ELEVEN

SPARED

The sun had not yet risen, but Chertney had already stood uncomfortably on a large rock below the walls of the Palace for several long hours. Around him soldiers ran around like worker ants, searching for Thomas' body. They had been there since the evening before, working through the night with nothing to show for it. Still, Chertney had not called off the search, and until he did, the soldiers would continue to perform their duties.

As he waited impatiently for some word on the boy, his mind drifted back to the previous night. Chertney had spent much of it with Rodric after his son's injuries were seen to. The slash across Ragin's arm had been deep, cutting into the bone. He had been lucky, though. The physick did not have to amputate the limb.

Ragin wasn't so lucky with his other wound, losing his right eye. Once the terrible wound healed, he would have to live with a large scar marring the right side of his face. A fate probably worse than death for someone like Ragin. Chertney could do nothing for the prince, as his talents did not lie in that direction. Nevertheless, no matter how many times he told Rodric that, the High King refused to believe him. And even if he could, he wouldn't. He did not waste his skills on arrogant fools.

After listening to Rodric rant and rave about what had happened for several hours, the High King frothing at the mouth as he worked himself into a rage, Chertney decided to take his leave and focus on the search. It wasn't going well, of course. As the hours passed, Chertney doubted they would find a body. A reasonable possibility was that the tide had pulled it out into The Gullet, but he doubted it.

Thomas had demonstrated a great deal of strength during the interrogation. Perhaps he had misjudged the boy even more than he originally believed. Perhaps the boy had the ability to mask his skill just as Chertney had. Chertney now had to admit to himself that the boy had hidden something from him. It was a possibility he didn't like thinking about. His master did not tolerate failure, especially at a time when his plans were moving forward so rapidly.

For the first time in centuries, Chertney knew fear. What he was about to do frightened him to the very core of his being. Stepping off the rock, he trudged back up to the main gate, ignoring the salutes of the soldiers he passed. Chertney was a visitor here, yet even they knew where the real power resided. Rather than heading toward the suite of rooms he occupied, he made for the steps leading down into the now-deserted dungeon, taking them two at a time despite the pitch black that greeted his eyes. He didn't need the light to see where he was going.

Chertney shut the door behind him as he entered the cell he had used to interrogate Thomas two nights before. He began immediately, not wanting to think about what he was about to do, and what the consequences of his actions might be. Otherwise, he might not have the courage to go through with it. Drawing on his Dark Magic, Chertney extended his power, searching for his true home, the home of his master. Searching for Shadow's Reach.

The blackness of the room took on a life of its own. A circular portal appeared before him, blacker than the darkness of the cell. The portal spun slowly at first, then faster, and faster still. Suddenly, it stopped, and a deathlike chill entered the room. Chertney immediately dropped to his knees and laid his head on the stone floor in submission.

"You have failed me, Chertney."

The voice was no more than a whisper, yet the chill of its tone sent a shiver of fear through Chertney. He felt an invisible, icy hand close around his heart. His breaths came in gasps.

"I tried, master. I truly did. But Rodric kept me from my task. Otherwise the boy would be dead."

There was a long silence. Chertney remained where he was, not daring to raise his head. The hand of cold tightened around his heart, probing, searching, finding everything his master wanted to know. No one could hide something from the Shadow Lord. Chertney shivered even more, fearing he was about to die.

"Rodric has become more of a problem," agreed the Shadow Lord. "I will have to do something about that."

Chertney breathed a sigh of relief, knowing that death had been forestalled, for now.

"The boy is still alive. I would have known if he had died." The Shadow Lord's voice was as dry as the dust in a tomb. "I will have to remedy that. We will speak on this further, Chertney. Until then, be ready. I will have need of you soon."

The darkness in the cell grew somewhat lighter as the spinning ball of black disintegrated. Chertney flopped down on the stone floor, savoring the natural cold that drifted into his body. He had been spared — for a time. He remained where he was for more than an hour, not wanting to go anywhere until the shivering he felt from the touch of the Shadow Lord had ended. He had been close to death before, but every time he spoke to his master, it was like he already had one foot in the grave.

Chapter Twelve

Found

Thomas heard a faint rustling in the woods off to his left, but he was too weak to turn his head and see what caused it. He had barely made it to the edge of Oakwood Forest, not far from where he had last met Kaylie and been taken, when he had lost control of the Talent. He had drained his strength to the point where only death was the next option. He closed his eyes for a moment, the simple task of keeping them open becoming too much for him.

"Thomas."

In an instant, Thomas opened his eyes. That voice—

"Thomas."

With some effort, Thomas slowly turned his head to the right and opened his eyes. Shock flowed through him, disbelieving what he saw.

"Grandfather?"

Talyn Kestrel stood before him surrounded by a ghostly aura, appearing just as he had the day Thomas fled the Crag. His grandfather rubbed his short, grey beard as he did when he was thinking or talking of something serious, yet the youthful gleam always remained in his eyes, even now.

"I'm here, Thomas. I'm here."

"But how? Am I dead?"

"No, Thomas," laughed Talyn. "Not yet. And with some luck, not for some time to come."

"Then why?"

Talyn stepped forward, kneeling by his grandson, his aura glowing brighter the closer he came.

"It is time, Thomas. It is time to stand on high."

Thomas looked at his grandfather in surprise. "But why now? Why has it taken so long?" His mind was a jumble of questions and emotions — guilt, joy and fear all mixing together.

"You had to see your true enemy, Thomas, before you could return to the Highlands," explained Talyn. "You know what you're up against now. You have that knowledge. And, more importantly, you know yourself — your strengths and weaknesses. It is time."

Talyn stood, looking down at Thomas with pride in his eyes.

"Use that knowledge. The Highlands are yours now. Take back what is yours. Free the Highlands and let loose the Marchers."

"But—"

In the blink of an eye Talyn vanished. Thomas closed his eyes, hoping that when he opened them again, Talyn would reappear. But as the seconds dragged into minutes, it became that much harder for him. He only wanted to sleep, and was about to drift off into the darkness when he felt a wet tongue on his face. When he opened his eyes again, Beluil grinned down at him.

"Hello, my friend," he said weakly, unable to raise an arm to pat the large wolf on the shoulder.

"It's about time," an irritated voice said behind him. "Do you know how long we've been looking for you?"

Thomas smiled. Rynlin came into view, kneeling beside him to check on his wounds. Next to him were Maden and Daran, and standing behind the two, Catal Huyuk. Beluil lay down next to Thomas. He had lost his friend once. He wasn't going to let him out of his sight this time.

"Grandfather, I—"

"Not a word, Thomas. We'll speak later. First drink this."

Thomas tasted the bitterness of the liquid as it passed his lips, reminding him of one of the concoctions Rya gave him when he was sick. In just a few seconds his eyes closed again and he drifted off to a deep, dreamless sleep.

"The boy has been through a lot," said Catal Huyuk.

"He has," replied Rynlin, taking out a cloth and sprinkling water from his canteen on it before dabbing around the wound on Thomas' side, and then his forehead, so he could see how badly Thomas was injured.

"I'm going to scout around. I'll be back in a few minutes."

Catal Huyuk disappeared among the trees. The large Sylvan Warrior felt the need to do something, and healing was not one of his specialties. His talents lay on the other side of the spectrum.

Maden helped Rynlin as they examined Thomas' wounds. Rya was going to have an absolute fit when she saw what had happened to her grandson. He'd have to get him to her first, though. Thomas was close to death, so he'd have to move fast.

"Events are moving very quickly," said Maden, as he sprinkled some herbs on the wound in Thomas' side. The bitterroot and sweet tooth would help stop the bleeding.

"They are," agreed Rynlin.

"Whoever did this to him probably knows about us."

"True," said Rynlin. "But there is nothing we can do about that now."

Maden nodded. "Is he ready?"

Rynlin knew the Sylvan Warrior was not asking about Thomas' condition to be moved. He stopped his ministering for a moment, looking Maden squarely in the eye.

"He is." Rynlin's pride was evident, and rightfully so, thought Maden.

Beluil growled just as Catal Huyuk burst through the trees, his sword covered in blood.

"Ogren," he said simply. "We'll have unwanted visitors soon."

"Blast it," cursed Rynlin, rising from his knees. "Let's get going."

Rynlin took hold of Thomas' shoulders and Maden grabbed his ankles, then lifted him off the ground and carried him deeper into the forest. Beluil and Catal Huyuk followed, alert for any new danger. They had a long way to go, and had only just begun.

Chapter Thirteen

Brightening Sky

The raptor circled the glade at the western edge of Oakwood Forest for some time, finally squawking in victory when the men appeared to help their injured comrade. The raptor sensed the spirit of the one below. He was more a part of nature than the world of man.

Satisfied that he would survive, the raptor wheeled to the northeast, its powerful wings pushing it through the air. As the hours passed and evening changed to night, so did the terrain. The forest gave way to the mountains of the Highlands.

The raptor twisted and turned around the majestic, snow-covered peaks, using the gusts of wind to propel itself through the thin mountain air. Eventually, as the sky began to glow a dark red, the raptor burst free of the mountains and flew across a lush, green valley, in the center of which rose an enormous monolith. Beating its wings furiously, the raptor climbed until finally it was level with the fast-approaching rock.

As the sun peeked above the eastern horizon, the raptor settled on the top of the monolith. An ancient fortress had once stood there, though now it was mostly reclaimed by the forest. However, part of one tower still stood, rising several hundred feet into the air. Perched on what had once been the Roost, the raptor turned its sharp eyes to the east, watching the rising sun brighten the Highland sky.

A cold wind blew across the plateau, and with it came a warning of impending darkness – and evil. Yet, the raptor knew that the light still burned brightly, and would burn even brighter, if the one chosen to wield it had the courage and strength to stand against the shadow.

Chapter Fourteen

Getaway

"They're gaining on us," said Catal Huyuk, even his strong voice coming with some effort.

He sat down heavily on a fallen tree. Ten-league walks didn't faze him, but even he felt the fatigue that also attacked his companions.

For most of the morning, he, Daran, Maden and Rynlin had fought a running battle with a band of Ogren and Shades sent to finish off Thomas. The Sylvan Warriors had found Thomas with the help of Beluil, the large black wolf with the splash of white over his eyes. The wolf now hovered over Thomas as Maden continued his efforts to staunch the flow of blood from the boy's many wounds.

Rynlin held one hand to his grandson's head, using the Talent to lend his own strength to Thomas. That was one of the reasons they were having such a hard time of it. With Rynlin and Maden occupied with Thomas, only he and Daran Sharban, the redheaded Sylvan Warrior, could focus their complete attention on the pursuing Ogren — and you wanted to focus your complete attention on Ogren, otherwise you died quickly.

The massive beasts were virtually unstoppable, leading to their favored role as the foot soldiers of the Shadow Lord. Ogren were twice the size of a man, their heavily muscled bodies covered by a thick, mangy fur. Because of their massive shoulders, some of the creatures walked hunched over, their backs unable to support the tremendous weight. The long, sharp tusks that protruded from their lower lips and curled in front of their cheeks made them appear even more menacing.

The beasts preferred to use huge axes, as swords and other weapons did not fit well in their hands. Some Ogren even wore armor, accumulating bits and pieces taken from their victims or from each other, though it truly wasn't necessary. Striking the skin of an Ogren was much like striking a rock, though when striking a rock you might slice off a piece. That rarely happened with Ogren.

Yet, the Ogren were the least of their worries, for leading their pursuers were at least three Shades – Catal Huyuk couldn't be sure how many there really were. He preferred calling them Shadowmen, or Snakemen, for that's what he thought they most resembled – the sinuous, graceful, deadly movements of a snake.

Legend said that Shades had once been men, but upon giving their souls to the Shadow Lord, something had changed within them. They resembled normal men, but their skin held a ghoulish cast and their eyes were a milky white. Beneath their black clothing, their bodies were gaunt and skeletal.

Rumor had it that they drank the spirit of their victims for nourishment. Catal Huyuk knew it for the truth. That's why he preferred fighting Ogren. At least with the large beasts you had a glimmer of a chance and could take advantage of their often awkward movements, while a single touch from the blade of a Shade meant instant death.

Catal Huyuk looked over to where Rynlin and Maden performed their ministrations. He was amazed that the boy even lived. Thomas' body had been pushed to the very limits of endurance. The cut on his forehead was the least of his problems. The slash to his side had allowed a dangerous amount of blood to escape, while the raw wounds left on his back from the bite of a whip sapped his strength and will to live. If not for Maden's medicinal skill and Rynlin's strength in the Talent, the boy would have died minutes after they had found him, lying in the grass in a small clearing at the western edge of Oakwood Forest.

"How far back?" asked Daran, who leaned against a tree, relishing the break.

He had expended a great deal of energy during the past few hours. The constant use of the Talent was taking its toll on him.

"A mile, two at the most."

Catal Huyuk had regained his breath. They had made it halfway through Oakwood Forest, but that wasn't far enough. To have any chance of throwing off pursuit, they needed to reach the Burren – a journey of at least another few hours, made all the more difficult since carrying Thomas on the makeshift stretcher they had built required two of them. And even then, they truly wouldn't be safe until they made it to the Isle of Mist, a journey of an additional few hours from the Burren.

"We must do something," said Maden, sitting down next to Thomas, done for the moment with his attempts to keep the wound on the boy's side from opening up once more.

If he lost more blood, their efforts will have been for naught. But that's something Maden didn't want to consider. Thomas was too important to their cause. Besides, Maden feared how such a result would affect the boy's grandfather. Rynlin had been devastated by the loss of his daughter years before. To lose Thomas— well, Maden chose not to think of it.

"But there is not much we can do," answered Rynlin, his attention still intent upon his grandson.

To break the bond by removing his hand meant Thomas would have to deal with his injuries on his own, something that would prove deadly in his current condition. Rynlin had spent the last few hours wracking his brain for a solution. Finally, he thought he had one.

"Perhaps Beluil could help us."

The large wolf jumped up at the mention of his name, having lain as close to his friend as possible. He and Thomas had grown up together, Thomas having found Beluil as a pup who had just lost his mother.

"Can you help us, Beluil?" asked Rynlin.

Beluil looked at Thomas' grandfather, the man's piercing green eyes reminding the wolf of his friend's own stare. In an instant the wolf disappeared into the brush.

"Hopefully he will succeed," said Rynlin. "In the meantime, I suggest we go."

The sounds of snapping branches and the guttural cries of the Ogren gave the Sylvan Warriors a new shot of strength. Catal Huyuk walked among the trees. He would lie in wait for their pursuers and try to slow them down. Daran picked up the stretcher at Thomas' head and Maden at his feet, with Rynlin maintaining contact with his grandson. They trotted to the north.

They could not go much farther, they all knew, but no one would say it aloud. They were Sylvan Warriors, guardians of the forest seeking to protect it from the evil of the minions of the Shadow Lord. One of their own was near death. They would continue for as long as they could, then face the consequences.

CHAPTER FIFTEEN

FAILURE

He was a short man with no distinct features, his coarse black hair and ruddy features suggesting peasant stock. He was much like anyone else in appearance. To make such a characterization in his presence, though, meant certain death.

Rodric Tessaril, High King and ruler of Eamhain Mhacha, brooked no insult, no matter how slight. With his less than dazzling appearance he could not afford to. To permit an insult, any insult, created the perception of weakness. And if someone, anyone, perceived you as weak, then, in fact, you were weak. He simply could not allow it.

That's why he went to such great lengths to ensure no one could mistake his status. He wore at all times a large, dark purple cape even though it dragged across the floor, and atop his head sat a heavy gold crown, often perched precariously since it was a bit too large for his head. Of course, no one had the courage to comment on his often comical appearance, choosing discretion – and life.

Rodric stood upon the dais in the throne room of the Palace, his arm resting on the golden chair that dominated the chamber. Once a reminder of the opulence and power of the Dunmoorian king, the throne room of Tinnakilly now represented the decay of the entire city. Paint strips hung from the ceiling, the faded wall hangings barely attached to their holders, the tiles in the floor more chipped and cracked than whole.

Rodric peered out one of the large windows at the cloudy, gray sky, thinking on the events of the past few days. His plans had been right on course, yet obstacles continued to appear in his path; some expected, others not, all dangerous.

"Still no sign of the boy?"

"No, milord," replied Lord Johin Killeran in a nasally voice.

He stood in front of the dais, not risking the High King's wrath by daring to step on it. Killeran rubbed his hands together nervously, an action that for once took attention away from his remarkably large nose. Though the Dunmoorian lord had slept little during the past three days, his breastplate was immaculate, as if the gleaming silver had been polished just minutes before he entered the room. Rodric decided it probably had. Killeran was nothing if not pompous and vain.

"Then keep looking."

"But, milord," began Killeran plaintively, stepping toward the High King, his nose leading the way. "We have searched the Gullet and the Pool and have found nothing. No one could have survived that fall, milord. No one. Even Chertney has said as much, believing that the body was pulled out by the current to Stormy Bay. There's no reason—"

Rodric wheeled on Killeran, his face bright red in anger, his eyes bulging, and his crown threatening to fall to the stone floor. His nose was less than a fingerbreadth from that of Killeran's.

"There is every reason, you fool. Every reason!"

The High King's shriek echoed in the chamber, making even the hardened soldiers who lined the walls tremble with fear. In a mood such as this, who knew how far, and at whose expense, the High King would go to assuage his temper.

"This boy represents the greatest possible threat to my plans. I want him killed, and if he's already dead, I want his head brought to me so I can confirm it with my own eyes. Do you understand me, Killeran?"

Killeran resisted the urge to wipe Rodric's spittle from his face. Instead, he nodded meekly in acquiescence.

"Yes, milord. We will continue the search until the body is found."

"Good," replied Rodric, stepping down from the dais and walking out through the massive doors, the hem of his robe catching the dust and dirt, darkening it even more. "Do not fail me in this, Killeran. I can't accept another failure on your part. Do you understand?"

"Yes, milord," said Killeran, bowing as the High King passed.

Killeran cursed Rodric silently as he left the room, resenting the power the small man held over him. He would do as commanded, even though he knew it would do little good. The boy couldn't have survived such a fall. It just wasn't possible. Still, this boy had proven his resilience before. Killeran would broaden the search, and hopefully he would find the body a bit further down the Gullet.

Resolved in his purpose, Killeran stared at the golden throne. It was enticing, its brilliance beckoning to him. One day, he promised himself. One day he would sit on that throne. One day he would finally get what he deserved.

CHAPTER SIXTEEN

DISFIGURED

Rodric strode purposefully down the crumbling hall, his boots crunching every now and then on the plaster falling from the deteriorating walls. Where was that fool Loris? He had demanded the presence of the King of Dunmoor more than an hour before, but the coward had not yet arrived. Probably hidden away in some whore's bed. He pushed his irritation to the side. There was still one more thing to tend to. Then he would deal with his erstwhile ally.

The two Armaghian soldiers stood at attention when the High King passed, bringing their halberds to their chests in salute. Rodric paid them no mind, intent instead upon what lay behind the doors that blocked his way.

Shoving open the heavy bronze doors, he stood on the threshold for a moment, allowing his eyes to adjust to the darkness. After a few seconds, he walked across the room and swept open the drapes. The gray light of the day turned the darkness into a gloomy murk, illuminating the bed set against the far wall.

Rodric walked over, the bile rising in his throat as he approached. The figure on the bed slept fitfully, having already discarded the blankets with his fevered movements. Rodric swallowed, sickened by the sight before him.

The gloom revealed the horrible wound running down the right side of his son's face. Ragin had been a fool to challenge the boy, not realizing that this Thomas was much like a cornered animal at the time, and thus much more dangerous.

Some would say that death was the ultimate price to pay. But with respect to his son, Rodric knew better. Silently he exited the room, pulling the door closed behind him. His son would have preferred death to disfigurement, for with this wound Rodric knew that in his mind Ragin had paid the ultimate price.

CHAPTER SEVENTEEN

RISING OF THE WOLVES

The wickedly curved axe came down in a vicious blow, sweeping off the Ogren's arm. The massive beast howled in agony, trying to escape. But the Ogren pushing from behind wouldn't allow it. Distracted by the horrible wound, the Ogren never saw the axe – one end a steel half-crescent, the other a half-foot steel blade – strike down once more. Biting into its neck, the monster died noisily.

Catal Huyuk tried to pull the blade free, the muscles in his arm bulging, but the steel had bit deeply and was wedged in the thick bone and muscle of the Ogren's neck. He sensed the other Ogren approaching, preparing to jump over the dead creature.

A knot of cold dread formed in his stomach. He didn't have time to free the blade! Desperate, he reached for the long daggers wedged into his belt. Another Ogren now stood over him, its terrifying maw spread into an even more frightening grin of bloodlust and pleasure. Catal Huyuk heard a shout from behind him.

"Down!"

He dropped to the ground, the ball of fire speeding through the space where he had stood just a half-second before. Another ball of fire came, and then another, and another. Each ball of fire struck an Ogren square in the chest, killing the creatures instantly. In one case, the fire was so hot it shot straight through one creature and struck another. Unable to withstand the assault, the Ogrens' attack faltered. The huge beasts fell back despite the orders of the Shades who stood a good distance back. The Sylvan Warriors had bought some more time.

Catal Huyuk rose wearily from the rocky ground, looking back to where Daran and Maden stood side by side, their stances and expressions mirroring his exhaustion. To have so much strength left to unleash balls of fire after such a long, continued use of the Talent was a testament to their power and abilities. Daran threw him a water bag, and he drank from it thirstily. He then pulled his axe free and wiped the blade clean on his torn cloak.

"Get what rest you can," Maden told his companions.

His ready smile had disappeared, replaced by a haggard expression. Though a sorcerer, he preferred leggings and jacket, much like Rynlin. He even wore a sword at his hip, though during the running battle of the last day he had relied on his skill with the Talent instead.

"The Shades will have the Ogren back under control and ready to attack in a few minutes."

None of the other Sylvan Warriors disputed his words. They had succeeded in reaching the southern edge of the Burren, but now they had to stop running.

The Ogren were too fast, and the beasts had almost encircled them. The Sylvan Warriors had fought their way through the trap, seeking refuge in a ravine that opened up into a small space that backed into a large stone outcropping. The Ogren couldn't attack from above or the sides, and only one of the creatures could come through the ravine at a time because of their great size.

If the Sylvan Warriors faced ordinary men, they could have held their position indefinitely, no matter the size of the attacking force. Such was not the case with Ogren. Yes, they could survive for a time, but when Maden and Daran tired to the point where they could no longer make use of the Talent, Catal Huyuk would be on his own. If Rynlin released his link with Thomas to join the fray, the boy would die. Then it would only be a matter of time, and they would have fought for nothing.

"They're coming!" shouted Daran, eyes no longer twinkling with their usual mirth.

Catal Huyuk retook his position in the middle of the ravine, hearing the thundering footsteps of the Ogren announcing their approach. He pushed back his long black hair from his face. The knot of leather he usually wore at the nape of his neck had been ripped from its place by a branch during their flight. Hefting his trusted axe, he realized the end likely would come soon.

"What was that?" asked Maden, his soft voice carrying easily through the enclosed space.

Catal Huyuk listened as well. Yes, he could hear something in the distance, but what? He couldn't place it.

He pushed it from his mind. He had business to attend to.

"Beluil succeeded," said Rynlin from farther back in the ravine, his sharp-featured face appearing almost gaunt because of the struggles of the past day, though his piercing green eyes still burned with determination. His hand remained on his grandson's forehead.

Thomas' condition had not changed during the entire journey, hovering close to death, held back only through his grandfather's strength and, as Catal Huyuk suspected, sheer will. Yet the effects of the bond began to show. Though Rynlin had not participated in any of the fighting, he appeared as tired and worn as his companions.

Catal Huyuk smiled evilly. He heard them now, the howls of the wolves drifting into the ravine. The Ogren heard the howls now too. That explained why the latest attack had stopped before it even began. There were few certainties with respect to nature, but one fact remained constant – wolves hated dark creatures, and given even the slightest opportunity, they would do whatever possible to kill the creatures of the Shadow Lord.

Catal Huyuk walked warily to the entrance of the ravine, making sure a sly Ogren did not lie in wait. His grin turned into a huge smile. Several hundred wolves had followed Beluil into battle — or perhaps slaughter was a better term. Half of the Ogren following after the Sylvan Warriors were already dead, lying on the ground in pools of their own blood. The remaining Ogren and Shades had a very short time to live.

The wolves had broken up into groups of four or five, each group surrounding a dark creature. The wolves did not attack rashly, instead waiting for the best chance. Then, when the opportunity presented itself, a single wolf would dart forward, seeking to hamstring its prey.

If the wolf failed, it stepped back, allowing one of its companions to try. It was really only a matter of time. The Shades were already dead, and the Ogren would last for only so long. As they tired they would make mistakes. Then they would die. The Ogren knew it, as did the wolves, whose attacks became bolder.

Beluil then appeared, trotting past Catal Huyuk to his friend, his nose bright red from dark creatures' blood. Catal Huyuk followed after. Thanks to Beluil and his friends, they would survive. And, more important, their effort had not been wasted. Thomas would live.

CHAPTER EIGHTEEN

NEW ADVERSARY

A chill wind swept across the crumbling balcony, swirling a thin layer of black dust into the air. The wind had no effect on the pitch-black cloak, which lay still, its folds impervious to the effects of nature. Finally, the bottom half of the cloak moved, responding to a shift in weight by the man wearing it. The only visible feature were his eyes — bright red eyes that burned with hunger.

"I am disappointed by Chertney's efforts," said the black-cloaked figure. "Very disappointed."

The voice came out as a hiss that held more danger than even that of a bloodsnake. The man continued to look out over the blackened city, which appeared to have been charred by a great conflagration, then to add insult to injury had suffered through an earthquake that ripped the ground apart and devastated most of the structures.

Few buildings remained whole in Blackstone, and those that did were beginning to feel the effects of time. Huge gaps and crevices crisscrossed the deserted city, which resembled the bottom of a dried-out lake baked by a desert sun.

"This boy is more of a problem than I expected. I thought Chertney would eliminate him with little trouble."

The shadowy figure finally turned away from the city to look at the tall, rail thin man who stood before him in the gray robes of a sorcerer. The bald man stared back, seemingly undisturbed by the burning orbs that met his gaze. There was no expression in the man's eyes, no feelings.

"I must adapt my plans, Malachias. I must move faster."

"Yes, master," replied Malachias, his dry voice devoid of emotion.

"You will not fail me, will you, Malachias?"

"No, master."

"For if you do, there will be a price to pay."

"Yes, master."

The threat washed off the gaunt Malachias, having barely any effect. He understood quite well the penalties for failure, having been given the privilege by his master several times to mete out necessary punishments to those who failed to serve the Shadow Lord as expected. And what fun that had been. A smile almost broke out on his face, but Malachias stopped it. Now was not the time to demonstrate his glee.

"Then go and do as I have commanded, Malachias. Show me that you deserve better than Chertney."

"Yes, master." In a blink of the eye, Malachias disappeared.

Malachias was stronger in Dark Magic than Chertney, as shown by his recent display, so that would give him an advantage, considered the Shadow Lord. Perhaps he had nothing to worry about after all. Still, after waiting all these years for the perfect opportunity, he could ill afford to leave any loose strings that could be used by his enemies.

The Shadow Lord turned back toward the dead city, taking pleasure in the gloom and murk that lay upon the land as far as the eye could see. There could be no loose strings. And if Malachias failed to cut off this one string, then he would have to take care of it himself.

CHAPTER NINETEEN

A DECISION

T homas Kestrel stood atop the cliffs of the Isle of Mist, looking out upon Shark Cove. Across the mile-long channel, the towering peaks of the Highlands rose upward, reaching for the cloudy blue sky, only to fall short by a hair. At the moment, though, Thomas' attention was directed downward. Beneath the cliffs in the frothy surf created by the incessant pounding of the waves against the rocky shore, the large fins of several Great Sharks tore through the sea.

The smallest of the adult Great Sharks grew to forty feet in length; the largest reached seventy feet. Adding the large, triangular, serrated teeth that were four or five inches in length confirmed the dominance of these creatures in their natural habitat. Yet different from other animals that killed to eat, the Great Sharks killed because they could, a remnant from their service to the Shadow Lord. These monsters of the sea swam in the deep waters of the ocean, though they favored a few places along the coasts, one of those being the aptly named Shark Cove.

Thomas watched as the Great Sharks swam gracefully through the sea and the frothy white waves struck the shore with their full power. Two forces of nature; one good, the other evil. It seemed as if the water tried to push the Great Sharks onto the shore, renouncing them to the land, but to no avail. It took quite a bit of effort for Thomas to draw his mind back to the reason he had come here in the first place.

The cool wind coming off the sea buffeted Thomas, and he pulled his dark green cloak tighter around his body. Even this far above the sea the misty spray created by the pounding surf dampened his short, brown hair, which curled in response to the wind's touch. Though his mind had wandered, his eyes shined brightly, mirroring the sharpness of his features.

There was a hardness to him, a seriousness you would not expect in one so young. When considering everything he had been through, and not yet having reached his twentieth birthday, his demeanor was quite understandable. Though not particularly tall, this quiet young man had an aura about him: one of purpose, determination, strength.

Thomas sighed softly, stroking his hand slowly through the scruff of Beluil's neck. The large black wolf sat contentedly beside his friend and enjoyed the distracted attention. Since escaping from Tinnakilly several months before, Thomas had recovered quickly. A slight scar was visible above his right eye, while a much larger one stretched along his side, a reminder of the Makreen's blade.

Even the many wounds crisscrossing his back had healed, though the scars remained. They ached from time to time, such as when it was about to rain – and during the dreams. No matter how hard he tried, at least once a week the nightmares came, a constant reminder of what he had experienced at the hands of the High King. In a way, it was useful. It strengthened his resolve.

He owed his grandfather and the other Sylvan Warriors his life. He had tried to tell Beluil the same thing, conversing with the wolf through his unique closeness to nature. The images Thomas created in his mind flowed into the mind of his furry friend, and from Beluil's mind into his. Once, certain people had been able to communicate with animals quite easily. Now, most everyone thought it a skill that had died out, or was no more than a legend, but such was not the case with Thomas.

Beluil had shrugged off Thomas' supposed debt, explaining that they were brothers. Brothers did such things for one another. No debt was involved. Besides, Thomas had done much the same when they had first become friends. Thomas chose not to argue. It was often a losing proposition with the stubborn wolf, who usually won most of their arguments by simply closing his eyes, rolling onto his side, and falling asleep.

Thomas looked out across the water separating the Isle of Mist from the western edge of the Highlands. He studied the snowcapped peaks, taking in their ruggedness, their enduring nature. It was time for him to make a decision, a decision that he had put off for some time. But he knew he couldn't wait any longer. Time was running short. Besides, he didn't really feel as if he had a choice. As his grandmother Rya liked to say, "You must do what you must do."

Almost ten years before, reivers and Ogren had entered the Crag through treachery. Though the Marchers fought bravely, they were outnumbered. With his father already dead, his grandfather had sacrificed his life so that Thomas could escape and carry on the traditions of the Kestrel clan. Thomas remembered the moment vividly, as he stood before the pitch-black opening of the escape tunnel, the sounds of battle and screams of death drawing closer.

"As a man, as a Kestrel Highlander, I give you these charges," Talyn Kestrel had said.

Thomas had suddenly felt something stir within him, an energy foreign to him. His blood had felt warmer as it sped through his veins.

"This is the sword of the Kestrels, the Sword of the Highlands," his grandfather continued. "I charge you to bring it to safety and to guard it with your life. When the time comes for you to become Lord of the Highlands, if it still may be so, you will have this sword at your hip."

Thomas now wore the blade in a scabbard across his back, the hilt visible above the neck of his cloak.

Talyn had continued with his orders as the steel blades of the Highland Marchers met the terrible onslaught of the Ogrens' axes. "My second charge is for you to remember. You are Thomas Kestrel, Lord of the Highlands upon my death, and I charge you to remember that, and to make sure that others remember it as well." His grandfather had then charged him to escape.

Reluctantly he had gone, entering the tunnel, knowing he would never again see his grandfather, the only person who to that point in his life had shown him any kindness, any love. Before the wall hiding the secret passageway swung back into place, Thomas had turned back toward his grandfather and with two hands hoisted the Sword of the Highlands into the air. He had yelled as loud as he could, "I am Thomas Kestrel, Lord of the Highlands! The Highlands will not be forgotten!"

His grandfather had replied, "For the Highlands!"

And then the stone wall had swung shut, enclosing Thomas in darkness. That memory had plagued him more and more during the last few months, visiting him far more regularly than he desired. Perhaps it was because time was slipping away.

Upon news of the reivers' attack on the Crag and the murders of Benlorin and Talyn Kestrel, the High King had tried to assume control of the Highlands. If not for Gregory of Fal Carrach's interference and demand that the law be followed, he would have succeeded. As the law required, when the ruler of a Kingdom died, and no true heir came forward, yet it could not be proven that all known heirs were dead, the High King must appoint a regent for a period of ten years.

Though the High King had tried to convince the assembled monarchs that the Kestrel line had come to an end, Gregory remained adamant. The grandson's body had not been found. Yes, he may have died in the attack, but if there is no body, there is no evidence of death. So it must be assumed that the grandson – Thomas – still lived.

If Thomas did not appear before the Council of the Kingdoms before the end of the decade-long period, in the eyes of the other monarchs he would lose his legal right to rule, and the High King, as prescribed by the law, would gain control of the Highlands. Rodric could then appoint a new ruler or, as Thomas suspected, take the Highlands for his own.

The ten-year period was almost at an end. At the next Council of the Kingdoms, slated for later in the year, if Thomas didn't declare himself Lord of the Highlands, Rodric would finally gain what he had lusted after for so long.

Thomas reached behind his head and pulled the Sword of the Highlands from the scabbard across his back. He examined it closely, despite having already memorized every inch of the blade. It was a plain sword, in the sense that there was very little in the way of ostentation – jewels weren't set in the hilt, nor gold inlaid in the grip. Yet it was an unmistakable sword, for on both sides of the blade where it met the hilt the Kestrel sigil was etched into the steel – a kestrel, soaring out of the sky, its claws outstretched for the kill.

He let the blade's point drop to the grass, and he once again looked out across the channel separating the Isle of Mist from the Highlands. Conflicting emotions fought within his heart, his mind having trouble making sense of the maelstrom. Yes, he had promised his grandfather that he would return and take his proper place among his people. But there was very little that he remembered while growing up in the Crag that made him want to return.

Most of the Highlanders living there had thought his mother a witch, noting the many strange things that seemed to happen around her. Thomas could never understand their fear, in part because his mother died so soon after giving birth to him.

While growing up the other children had teased him mercilessly, focusing on his bright, green eyes. They called him a goblin, a ghoul. That's why he wandered alone through the forests beneath the Crag so much, enjoying the solitude of his private excursions. The animals never accused him of anything, and because of his special skill, they accepted him for what he was.

The only one who had shown any love for him at the Crag was his grandfather. Talyn would come to his room to read him stories and teach him the history of the Highlands. That was the only time he felt like he belonged in the Crag, when he was in the company of his grandfather. A sadness he had thought long gone welled up within him. He had come to grips with his grandfather's death many years before, but the pain remained.

And what of his responsibilities as a Sylvan Warrior? Nothing in life had felt as good as the moment he passed the challenges to become a Sylvan Warrior. Even with the forbidding future that lay before him, he would have done it all over again in a second.

Serving as a Sylvan Warrior made him feel complete, as if he were doing what he was born to do. The closeness he felt to nature was the greatest sensation he had ever experienced. That and the pleasure that surged through him upon dispatching another of the Shadow

Lord's minions. Would returning to the Highlands keep him from his duties as a Sylvan Warrior?

Still, he could not ignore the need of his people. Rynlin and Rya had said many times before that he would know when it was time to return to the Highlands and take his proper place, but doubts still plagued him, even with his vivid memories of his time as a prisoner in the Black Hole. His capture by Killeran had opened his eyes to the suffering of his people.

Killeran had done his best to enslave as many Highlanders as possible, all in his quest to extract as much gold and other minerals from the Highland mines. Though the Highlands was a rugged and dangerous land, beneath its surface lay more wealth than could be found in all the other Kingdoms combined.

Thomas remembered the faces of the gaunt, weak men, women and children herded into their cages to spend another night weighed down by their misery and sorrow. His guilt at doing nothing to protect his people had almost overcome him, yet reason won out. He could not have done anything to prevent what had happened, but he could help his people now.

And he had, by freeing his people, burning down the Black Hole, and decimating Killeran's troops. His actions gave hope once again to the Highlanders. Should he not finish the job? Yes, his people were stronger now, but if Rodric gained control of the Highlands, eventually they would be wiped out, and most of the other Kingdoms wouldn't care. He simply could not allow that to happen.

And what of the visit by Talyn's spirit? Thomas had lain close to death in the glade at the western edge of Oakwood Forest upon his escape from Tinnakilly when the spirit of his long-dead grandfather had suddenly appeared. Every night since then his grandfather's words had played through his mind: "It is time, Thomas. It is time to stand on high."

Thomas had looked upon the spirit in surprise.

"But why now?" he had asked. "Why has it taken so long?"

"You had to see your true enemy, Thomas, before you could return to the Highlands," his grandfather had replied. "You know what you're up against now. You have that knowledge. And, more importantly, you know yourself – your strengths and weaknesses. It is time."

Talyn had then looked down at him with pride in his ghostly eyes.

"Use that knowledge. The Highlands is yours now. Take back what is yours. Free the Highlands and let loose the Marchers."

It is time. Thomas raised the Sword of the Highlands once more. In addition to the twin kestrels, an inscription ran along the steel of the blade: "Strength and courage lead to freedom."

Perhaps the inscription applied directly to him. Did he have the strength and courage to be free? Ever since his escape from the Crag one responsibility after another had bombarded him, to the point where he felt like he had no control over his life. Perhaps that's why his grandmother's favorite saying – "You must do what you must do" – grated on him.

But maybe this was a way to break free of his responsibilities. If he succeeded in what he needed to do, he could regain some control over his life. The question remained, though. Did he have the strength and courage to be free? Thomas returned the blade to its scabbard. It was time to find out.

CHAPTER TWENTY

FOR DUTY

As Thomas walked down the narrow path leading away from the cliffs, Beluil trotted before him. The wind had picked up, bringing with it an added bite announcing that autumn was settling across the north. Yet it felt different than previous seasons, with a sharper cold settling over the land. Though Beluil had proven himself time and again against Ogren and other menacing creatures – a testament to his toughness — he enjoyed certain luxuries, such as curling up in front of the fire on a cold, windy night. Thomas let him go ahead, still caught up in his thoughts.

"How long have you been waiting?" Thomas asked, not bothering to look up.

He had left the beach and entered the forest of heart trees that dominated the Isle of the Mist. Heart trees were the largest in all the Kingdoms, some rising several hundred feet into the sky with their trunks fully a hundred feet around. The roots of these legendary trees snaked across the forest floor, with many large enough for Thomas to walk under.

Once, millennia before, heart trees had stood from one end of the Kingdoms to the other, when the men and women who lived on the continent still had some understanding of nature and its role in the world. But no more. Those that remained survived within the Highlands and on the Isle of Mist. It was said that if you placed your ear against the bark of a heart tree, you could hear the beating of the earth's heart. Thomas knew it to be true, but he had an advantage most everyone else did not.

His grandfather rose from his seat on the gnarled root of a heart tree.

"Not long," replied Rynlin Keldragan, stretching his long frame.

Rynlin was one of the tallest men Thomas had ever met, and with his sharp features, short black beard flecked with grey, piercing green eyes, and intense gaze, he had a dastardly, menacing appearance. It was a persona that Rynlin rather enjoyed.

"I was just finishing my circuit of the island, making sure all my surprises were still intact."

He fell in beside his grandson as they navigated the heart tree roots on their way home.

"When was the last time one of your surprises was actually needed?"

Rynlin was silent for a time, as he could not recall immediately.

"Before you came here," he replied. "Maybe fifteen years? I can't remember exactly."

Rynlin shook his head as if he were frustrated.

"It's a bit disappointing, really. Though your grandmother and I have never liked being disturbed, when we did have uninvited guests, it was a great deal of fun watching them go," said Rynlin, revealing his mean streak.

Rynlin was not the type of person you wanted to irritate or anger. He never forgot, and sometimes waited hundreds of years to exact retribution.

Thomas smiled to himself as his grandfather fell silent. He remembered the first time Rynlin had explained the many surprises that awaited those trespassing on their island. For centuries, legend had it that hidden upon the Isle of Mist were untold riches from the many treasure chests buried there by the pirates who used to roam the Sea of Mist.

No one had ever confirmed if the legends were anything more than that, but there were always men willing to take risks for what they perceived to be the easy acquisition of gold and jewels. So bands of treasure hunters journeyed to the Isle of Mist from time to time in search of an easy fortune. When Rynlin and Rya made the Isle of Mist their home, they decided to dissuade these ne'er-do-wells.

In the taverns of the eastern coast, Rynlin began planting rumors about the horrors of the Shadowwood – the name that he had come up with for the forest on the Isle of Mist. Then, if the fortune seekers were too stupid to ignore the legends that Rynlin created, they often met with a nasty surprise soon after landing on the island, courtesy of Rynlin and Rya's skill in the Talent.

Rynlin took a special pleasure in watching the bravest of men run in terror from the Shadowwood, more often than not diving into the surf and swimming for their ships, not wanting to wait for the landing boats to pick them up. Sometimes that was a mistake. If they swam in the wrong direction, they became bait for the Great Sharks, but that was the price you often paid for greed.

Thomas wore an evil grin as he and Rynlin approached their home. He and his grandfather were more alike than either cared to admit. As they made their way through the heart trees, a door opened in the trunk of one only a few feet before them. To anyone who did not know what to look for, this particular heart tree resembled all the others. But for Rynlin, Rya and Thomas, it was home. Beside the door, several windows were carved into the tree, and halfway up its massive trunk, a chimney allowed the smoke of the fire to escape.

Following Thomas over the threshold, Rynlin remembered to lower his head just before it knocked into the top of the door frame, something that happened with an all too common frequency, thought Rya, as she shut the door behind her husband and grandson. Rynlin had a tendency to forget certain things, though slights and insults were not among them.

He also had something of an ego. When he first carved the house from the tree, he had never considered that he could have made a mistake in the size of the door. He had been paying for that mistake in bruises and headaches ever since. So, all in all, Rya thought it was a good thing for her husband – it helped to keep him humble, just the way she liked him.

Rya was barely five feet tall, and next to her husband appeared even smaller, but she had a commanding presence. Her dark chestnut hair and deep blue eyes had captivated many a man when she was young, yet it was her mettle that had first drawn Rynlin to her. She preferred to view herself as strong-willed; Rynlin chose another term – bullheaded – but rarely used it in her presence.

"What have you been doing, Thomas?" Rya asked.

She walked over to the fireplace, a wooden spoon in hand. After pulling the pot away from the flames, she stirred the stew slowly, making sure their dinner didn't burn.

Vegetable stew, Thomas realized, as the smell wafted through the kitchen.

"Thinking," he replied.

Thomas took his place at the table and thanked his grandmother for the bowl filled with a thick gravy and large pieces of carrots, potatoes, beans and other tasty morsels. His grandparents joined him.

"About what?" she asked, hesitant to go any farther.

She knew what Thomas pondered. It had dominated his thoughts for the last few months. A part of her knew that it was time, but another part of her, the one that still viewed Thomas as the little boy he had been when he had first come into their lives, dreaded that this day had come. Rya did her best to remain calm.

"You know as well as I," Thomas replied softly.

Rynlin stopped eating, his bowl still half full. He was not one to let a good meal go to waste, but though he didn't like to admit it, he too had dreaded this moment.

"What have you decided, Thomas?"

He knew the answer – at least he thought he did – but he needed to hear the words.

Thomas breathed deeply, trying to calm the butterflies that threatened to explode from his stomach. He knew how his grandparents were going to react.

"It's time. I can't put it off any longer. My people need me."

Rynlin and Rya stared at him, neither saying a word. Thomas had expected yelling or a lecture on responsibility, or perhaps something on considering all sides of an issue before making a decision. Not stony silence.

Finally, Rynlin settled back in his chair. "We knew this day would come, Thomas. I'm sure your grandmother would agree that we weren't looking forward to it, but as I said, we knew it would come."

Thomas nodded. He knew how difficult this was for them. When Thomas had become a Sylvan Warrior, he had, theoretically, become an adult, and had gained the freedom to wander the Highlands as was required by his duties among the Sylvana. But this decision went beyond that. It meant that Rynlin and Rya would no longer be able to offer guidance as they had when he was younger. They could do nothing to help him in this.

"There is an old saying, Thomas. If men cannot master war, war will master them. The same could be said for revenge."

Thomas gazed intently at Rynlin. At first he had thought to respond harshly, rising to Rynlin's bait. But Thomas quickly realized that would have been a mistake. As his grandfather had done so many times in the past, Rynlin tested him.

"I go not for revenge, but for a promise, for duty. The Highlanders never had any use for me when I was growing up in the Crag, but I can't allow that to color my judgment. That doesn't matter anymore. I am a Highlander. I must help my people."

Rynlin nodded, satisfied by the response. Tears appeared in Rya's eyes, but she wiped them away. She too approved. It was time for him to live his own life, and to succeed or fail based on his own decisions. It was time to return to the Highlands. But that didn't mean she had to like it.

CHAPTER TWENTY-ONE

A LOSS

The tall man placed his feet carefully, using his spear as a walking stick. The rocks lining the path were loose until you reached the plateau, meaning a single slip could lead to a deadly fall. Reaching the crest, he took a moment to enjoy the sight of the rugged peaks rising into the sky, the distance between each one covered by pine, fir and evergreen trees. He breathed in the sharp, cold air.

He had traveled the Armagh Mountains hundreds of times – as was his wont and his responsibility. As a Sylvan Warrior, Aurel was charged with protecting nature against the evil of the Shadow Lord, something he had done for several centuries. He had never tired of the task. In fact, he relished it. His duty gave him a pleasure that few other people would ever know.

On the other side of the plateau lay a wider trail that led higher up the mountain and then down to the plain he would have to cross to reach Branaeil, the city nestled between the Three Fork River and the Heartland Lake. He rarely visited cities, preferring the solitude of the forest, but sometimes you didn't have a choice. He was halfway across the plateau when he realized that he was being hunted. Aurel cursed himself for a fool. He should have felt the approaching evil sooner, but his mind had wandered.

Stopping on the path, he took hold of his spear with both hands, slowly circling around in an effort to locate the source of his discomfort. The hairs on the back of his neck straightened. The evil was getting closer, much closer. He had fought in hundreds of battles and skirmishes against some of the most terrifying creatures ever to leave Shadow's Reach, yet he had never really gotten used to the fear and uncertainty he felt right before the struggle began.

The anticipation of it all was the worst part of it. As Aurel continued to circle, scanning the brush that lined the edge of the plateau, the sense of approaching evil grew stronger. It seemed as though it was coming toward him from several directions. That could only mean—

Two Fearhounds burst from the foliage to his left, their long strides eating up the space between them and their quarry in heartbeats. The size of ponies, the Fearhounds were the color of night. It was rumored that once Fearhounds had gotten the scent, they never failed to catch their prey, for their skill was not in hunting by sight, or scent, but rather by fear, sensing it in their quarry.

The analytical side of Aurel's mind noted that fact, which meant he simply hadn't run into them. No, they were sent after him. That was the only explanation. The instinctual part of Aurel's mind brought the spear around, ready for the charge. The Fearhounds large teeth, which extended beyond their lower jaw, and hot saliva dripping from their gaping maws intensified their fearsome appearance. There was only one way to kill a Fearhound, Aurel knew, as their thick skin was like the bark of a heart tree – almost impregnable. He would have to strike true.

As the first Fearhound came within range, having outdistanced the other beast, Aurel's spear shot out. The sharp point tore through the creature's eye and into its brain, killing it instantly. He immediately pulled the spear free and directed it toward the other Fearhound. Though the beast had seen its companion fall, its bloodlust hastened its charge, relying on its speed for a sure kill. Once again Aurel's aim was true, the spear striking through the eye and killing the beast.

He tried to work the blade free, but it was lodged too deeply. He could sense other Fearhounds on the plateau now, charging, taking advantage of his weakness. He pulled with all his strength but the spear wouldn't budge. Reaching for the long knife in his belt, he swung the blade behind himself in a deadly arc, catching another Fearhound across the throat.

Such a slash would have killed any other beast instantly, but not a Fearhound. The creature barely felt the wound and continued with its attack, its weight knocking Aurel to the ground. He tried to rise, but before he could a fourth Fearhound was on him, crushing one of his legs in its powerful jaws. The pain almost overwhelmed him, yet Aurel still tried to defend himself, bringing the long knife up in an attempt to dislodge the two Fearhounds.

As the blade came down, aimed for the back of the creature that had bitten his leg, a fifth Fearhound arrived, its jaws nearly severing his hand from his wrist. And then the rest of the pack appeared. It was over in a matter of seconds. When the lapdogs of the Shadow Lord had finished with the body, it was barely recognizable. The only distinguishing feature was a silver amulet inscribed with the horn of a unicorn shining brightly as it caught the rays of the early morning sun.

CHAPTER TWENTY-TWO

HINT OF MADNESS

"You were a fool," hissed Rodric, throwing the drapes back to allow the sun to stream into the musty room.

Not much had changed since Rodric had brought his son back to Armagh. Ragin lay on the bed, his head resting on the stone wall. His face twisted into an angry glare at his father's words, made all the more fearsome by the fresh scar running from his scalp to his neck on the right side of his face. A bandage still covered where his eye had once been, and strewn around the room were dozens of different patches, none of which had yet met with the Prince of Armagh's approval.

"He got lucky!" Ragin screamed back at his father. "If I had killed him it would have furthered your plans and given me the respect I deserve. I—"

"But you didn't kill him," said Rodric, standing before his son. "You embarrassed yourself and, worse, you embarrassed me."

Rodric began pacing the room, stopping to open a window. Ever since they had returned from Tinnakilly months before, his son had stayed holed up in his rooms living in a world of semidarkness. He had ordered the servants to remove all the mirrors, not wanting to be reminded of the terrible wound that had marred his once handsome features.

"In fact, we don't even know if the fall killed him," continued Rodric. "His body was never found."

"I hope he survived," whispered Ragin, a small smile creeping onto his face, which, combined with the scar, gave him an almost grotesque appearance. "Then I can pay back the pain and suffering he has caused me."

"You're even more of a fool than I thought!" shouted Rodric, rounding on his son. "The boy was injured and weak, yet he still bested you with a blade. If you meet him again and he's at full strength, you'll simply be giving him the opportunity to finish the job he started."

"I said he was lucky, blast you! The next time—"

"Enough!" Rodric slapped his son across the face, needing an outlet for his growing anger.

Ragin flinched under the blow, a hint of madness touching his eyes. He wished desperately for a dagger. Someday his father would pay for that. Some day.

"I have no time for your outbursts. Because of you, I've had to rework my plans. And that's taken time I can ill afford to lose with the Council of the Kingdoms only six months away. You have a simple choice. Do you plan to cower here in fear, or will you help me with what needs to be done?"

"Leave me alone!" screamed Ragin, spitting the words out of his mouth. "I don't want to be seen! Can't you understand that?"

Rodric moved back from the bed, looking down at his son in disgust. He had been wrong. His son wasn't just a fool, he was a coward. He had no time for fools or cowards or, more importantly, people who no longer fit into his plans.

"Fine," he said, heading for the door. "I'll make sure you get your wish."

CHAPTER TWENTY-THREE

FIXATION

The steel blade whipped out, searching for an opening. Steel was met with steel, though muted by the pieces of leather covering the blades, turning away the blow. Kaylie stepped back for a moment, wiping long strands of black hair from her sweaty brow. The practice session with Kael Bellilil, Swordmaster of Fal Carrach, had lasted for more than an hour, much of that the result of her abilities. But Kael would never tell her that. Not yet, anyway. She was becoming a fine fighter, but he didn't want her to become overconfident.

Kaylie crouched once more, circling her opponent slowly. Kael simply watched and waited, allowing her to be the aggressor. Ever since Tinnakilly they had met in the practice yard at the end of the day, with Kael instructing the princess in how to use a blade. She was a spirited girl — and stubborn. You could see it in her deep blue eyes. There was a confidence there now and a purpose that had been lacking until only recently.

Only months before she had simply accepted her role as Princess of Fal Carrach, unwilling to push too far beyond the comfort of what she was familiar with.

But no more. As a result of recent events she had discovered a whole new world – one of danger, betrayal and love. Though she'd never admit the last to herself, Kael knew the truth of it.

She was also very intelligent and had learned quickly to use her petite size and speed to her advantage. As if his thoughts were a signal, Kaylie darted forward, her sword aimed for Kael's knee. Smart and clever. Disable a larger opponent, then move in for the kill. It had been one of his first lessons.

Kael grinned as his sword deflected the blow, then came back up immediately as Kaylie tried to catch him unawares with a strike to his arm. The clang of steel on steel continued for several minutes as the two combatants made use of every inch of the practice yard in their struggle. With the sun almost below the trees to the west, Kael decided it was time to stop.

"Enough, Princess. We can continue tomorrow."

Kaylie reluctantly ended her attack, allowing the exhaustion she experienced after each practice session to take hold of her body. It was a good feeling, one of accomplishment and success.

"Fine," she grumbled. "Tomorrow then."

"You know, Princess, you've come a long way in a very short time," Kael said. "Just make sure you don't lose sight of the larger picture."

Kael sat heavily on one of the benches that marked out the practice area, unwrapping the leather from his blade. He had the grizzled appearance of a veteran, which was confirmed by the scar running halfway across his neck.

"What do you mean?" asked Kaylie, sitting next to the Swordmaster and beginning the same process of freeing her steel blade.

"You know very well what I mean," answered the bald Swordmaster. "You have focused almost all of your attention on learning the sword during the last few months, to the exclusion of almost everything else. I know why you're doing it, girl, but at some point it's not going to be enough. You're going to have to move on."

Kaylie sighed resignedly. Leave it to Kael to see through her so easily.

"But it's what's been keeping me going," she replied. "Every time I think of what happened—"

"Stop beating yourself up, girl," interrupted Kael, using the tone so familiar to the newest recruits in the Fal Carrachian military, a tone they dreaded. "Don't forget, girl, a body was never found. That Thomas was a tough one."

"But no one could survive a fall from—"

"You've said it yourself many times. He had special skills. What's done is done. It's time to move on. You need to see everything that's going on around you, not just a small part of it. You won't be the swordfighter you can be – the leader you need to be — until you do."

Satisfied that his message had gotten through, Kael rose from the bench and walked toward the armory. He wanted the blacksmith to work out some of the nicks in his blade.

Kaylie watched him go. She stayed there until well after dark, thinking on Kael's words. She knew he was right. It was time to move on. But could she?

Chapter Twenty-Four

Moving Forward

Thomas felt the rush of air that came off the mountains, buffeting him, trying to force him down. His strong wings carried him onward, undeterred by the mighty blasts. Using the Talent to change himself into a kestrel, he now flew several thousand feet above the land.

He wasn't sure what kind of reception he would receive at Raven's Peak. He had chosen the village carefully. Oso lived there now, his best friend among the Highlanders. Coban also lived there. The former Swordmaster of the Highlands, best friend to his grandfather, Talyn, would know what needed to be done. Also, many of the people he had rescued from the Black Hole now resided in the village situated high in the upper passes of the Highlands, several days west of the now destroyed Crag.

Worries plagued him as he navigated around the Highland peaks. Thomas had waited almost ten years before returning home. Why should the Highlanders even care? Why should they feel any allegiance to an outsider? More to the point, though Thomas had tried to help his people as best he could – freeing Oso and the other Highlanders from the Black Hole, eliminating as many dark creatures and reivers as possible during his frequent wanderings through his homeland as part of his responsibilities as a Sylvan Warrior – they had suffered quite a bit since the Crag fell.

Would Coban and Oso support his claim? Would the people of Raven's Peak? While growing up the Highlanders had always perceived Thomas as different and had treated him that way when he lived in the Crag, accepting him only because he was Talyn's grandson. In fact, rumors had circulated throughout the Highlands; rumors that Benlorin Kestrel would one day remarry and have more children. Then the Highlanders wouldn't have to worry about having a witch's brood ruling them. Did his people still feel that way?

His people. It was a strange concept to Thomas, one he had never really considered before. True, he was a Highlander, his lineage going back for centuries, to the very time when the Highlanders carved out their own Kingdom. But he had never felt as if he belonged, as if he truly were a Highlander.

As his worries slowly simmered into budding fears, a screech to his right broke Thomas' train of thought. A female kestrel flew beside him. Thomas studied the beautiful bird for a moment. He had seen the kestrel before, remembering the sharp eyes, eyes that seemed to peer into the very depths of his being, examining his fears and his worries. For some strange reason he sensed the kestrel had been with him all his life, watching, waiting, knowing there would come a time when Thomas would finally understand who he was. Though the kestrel seemed to know, and had always known, Thomas still searched for that knowledge.

They flew in silence for a time, every one of Thomas' glances meeting the steely eyed glare of the other kestrel, almost as if the large bird of prey escorted him to his destination – and so he didn't turn around, succumbing to his fears. When the palisade surrounding the village finally came in sight, the other kestrel turned away, but not before it let out a screech that echoed off the surrounding mountainsides.

Since Thomas had assumed the form of the kestrel in order to make his traveling easier and faster, he had also assumed many of the instincts of the kestrel, which allowed him to read more into the kestrel's cry than he would have normally. It was almost as if the female kestrel was letting go, allowing Thomas to fly on his own now. The kestrel's message was quite simple: *Be strong. Be true.*

Those words echoed through his mind as he descended into the forest, bolstering his courage. He settled into a small clearing a half-mile from the village, then released his hold on the Talent. The shape of the kestrel fell away and his own figure returned.

Checking to make sure he had everything he needed, Thomas trotted through the forest. He had often wondered what happened to his clothes and weapons when he assumed the kestrel form. His grandparents, usually so ready and willing to give him advice and lectures, had offered little information, with Rya telling him in a slightly embarrassed tone that she didn't know.

Thomas didn't have to worry about Highland scouts this close to Raven's Peak. He could sense the men Coban had sent out as sentries farther away, patrolling specific territories in overlapping circles, ensuring the people of the village would have ample warning if reivers approached. Leaving the forest for the trail a few hundred feet from his destination, he was almost to the gates when a familiar voice rang out.

"It certainly took you long enough to get here. I've been waiting for months."

Momentarily worried that someone had discerned his true intentions, Thomas was immediately put at ease when he saw the large Highlander trotting toward him. Oso grabbed his smaller friend into a bear hug, sucking out Thomas' breath. Oso was almost as tall as Rynlin, but Rynlin appeared small next to Oso because of the boy's broad shoulders and large frame.

"You've got to be more careful, Oso," said Thomas. "One of these days you're going to crush someone."

"Sorry," his friend replied sheepishly.

Thomas laughed softly, unable to resist taking a small bite.

"What if it were Anara? Do you squeeze her that hard when you're kissing her?"

Oso's face turned flaming red, and he kicked at the dirt in consternation. "Thomas, please?"

Oso's pained expression was that of a man caught in a trap, and not at all certain that he wanted to escape — and even if he could, how to do it.

"I've been waiting for months for you to return so we could hunt and I could get away from jokes like that."

Now it was Thomas' turn to apologize. "I'm sorry, Oso. I just couldn't resist. Where is Anara anyway? I would have expected her to be attached to your side?"

Ever since the two had met in the Black Hole, Anara had woven her web around the large Highlander, and then, as time passed, slowly, ever so slowly, she had begun to tighten it. Oso had been completely and utterly trapped, not even realizing what she was doing to him.

Oso ignored the playful jibe as he led his friend through the gates and into Raven's Peak.

"She said she had to take care of some business, and I really didn't want to know what she meant."

Thomas had a feeling he knew exactly what Anara had meant, but he decided that he had had enough fun at his friend's expense, so he kept his thoughts to himself.

"But this is perfect timing on your part. With Anara occupied, just give me a few minutes. I'll get my bow and we'll be off. She won't realize where I've gone for at least two or three days. Just enough time for us to enjoy some good hunting."

Appealing as that sounded to Thomas, he reluctantly begged off.

"I'm sorry, Oso. Unfortunately, I'm here because I have some business that I need to attend to as well. Where's Coban?"

Oso studied his friend for a moment, trying to figure out Thomas' intentions. He couldn't read Thomas' calm and unfathomable expression. However, Thomas' eyes burned brightly. If it was night, they would have glowed a dark green. Oso had seen that expression before and knew better than to ask any questions. Thomas would tell him when it was time. Pushing his own desires to the side, Oso began walking deeper into the village.

"Follow me, Thomas. I'll take you to him."

Chapter Twenty-Five

A Declaration

"I'm surprised to see you, Thomas. I thought Oso would have kidnapped you and taken you off on a hunting trip as soon as you set foot in the village."

Coban sat back in his favorite rocking chair in front of a dark fireplace. Soon he would have to make use of it. The weather was getting colder. But that wasn't what made the hair on the back of Coban's neck prickle. He sensed something important was about to happen. What it could be, he didn't know. Anticipation began to build within him for some unknown reason.

"He tried," Thomas replied.

Thomas surveyed the small, comfortable cottage. Besides the larger room they now occupied, a darkened doorway led to a small bedroom. Everything in the cottage was neat and orderly, mimicking the man who lived there.

Thomas had spent barely any time with the Swordmaster before the fall of the Crag, as most Highland boys didn't begin weapons training until their eleventh summer. However, Coban had never treated him like the others, whether out of respect for his grandfather or simply because he had a broader mind than most everyone else, Thomas never asked. He simply appreciated being treated like everyone else, rather than as an outcast.

Looking back now, the fact that he hadn't spent much time with Coban was a good thing. After helping Oso and the others escape from the Black Hole, he had led them here, to Raven's Peak. Thomas had worried that Coban would recognize him, and then Thomas would have no choice but to move forward on the path he was now on before he was ready.

Thankfully, Coban hadn't made the connection, though at the time Thomas could see in Coban's eyes that there was a flicker of recognition. Thomas counted on that flicker now to aid him on the quest he was about to embark on.

"What was it like before the murder of Talyn Kestrel, Coban? What was it like for the Highlanders?"

Coban looked at the serious young man seated before him for a moment, somewhat unprepared for the question as it opened a floodgate of locked away memories. He was about to ask why Thomas wanted to know, but chose not to. Oso had told Coban stories about Thomas' eyes, about how they could burn with such an intensity it would mesmerize you or terrify you, depending on if you were friend or foe. Thomas' sharp green eyes burned like that now.

"It was a time of glory," he began, leaning back into his chair and staring up at the rafters supporting his roof. A small smile crept onto his face. He leaned forward suddenly, catching Thomas up in his tale from the start.

"Now, most anyone could say that about a ruler now gone, and most do, I'll grant you that. But I speak truly about this. Talyn had ruled for more than two decades, and during that time the Highlands had flourished. Though we were small in number, we were the best fighters in all the Kingdoms. And, most important, the other Kingdoms knew it, so they left us in peace.

"That hadn't always been the case, as I'm sure you know. The Highlands holds a great many riches – gold, jewels, precious minerals – and many of the other rulers certainly envied our wealth, but they knew the price they would pay if they entered our lands uninvited."

"Now you see, lad, before Talyn there wasn't much order to the Highlands," continued Coban. "As a result, some of the other Kingdoms would risk sending in a mining party for the opportunity at a quick fortune, but that ended when Talyn became Lord of the Highlands. In other Kingdoms, the tradition is that the ruler, monarch, whatever he or she is called, owns all the land, and the people of the Kingdom farm it, live on it, do whatever with it, at the ruler's pleasure. It can be taken away from them at any time for any reason and they have no recourse."

Thomas settled back into his rocking chair, allowing his mind to drift. He knew much of what Coban was explaining to him, but he had asked the question for two reasons. First, he needed some additional time to gather his thoughts and think of a way to broach the discussion's true topic with Coban. Second, he wanted to make Coban feel comfortable. Judging by Coban's animated gestures and his zest for the tale, it was working.

"Such is not the case in the Highlands. The people own the land; the Lord of the Highlands owns nothing except the lands surrounding the Crag. That was primarily done so the Lord would have some way to provide for the people residing in the Crag and his Marchers. But Talyn came up with an ingenious plan. In return for protection from the reivers and others seeking the wealth of the Highlands, those Highlanders who owned the mines gave to the Lord of the Highlands a percentage of what they mined. It was also an excellent way to keep my Marchers in good fighting form.

"Talyn then let it be known that anyone daring to enter the Highlands without permission would face the most severe consequence. After a few examples were made, the treasure hunters took it very seriously. We were the strongest of all the Kingdoms, lad, and everyone knew it. We were at peace, trade flourished, and our people didn't have to worry about war or famine. Unfortunately, with Talyn's murder, it all came to end."

Coban sighed resignedly. "I'd give anything to go back to those days, lad. Anything."

Thomas had finally decided on a way to bring up the main topic for discussion. He hoped he got the result he so desperately wanted.

"How was it that Talyn Kestrel came to be Lord of the Highlands?"

"Like it had happened for centuries before him," replied Coban, leaning back in his chair once again.

He could feel the chill of the day now as the sun approached the western horizon. He should have started that fire.

"Normally the title fell from father to son, from one family to the next. If a Highland Lord died without an heir, it went to the family with the strongest claim. But, keep in mind that we Highlanders have always had the right to refuse a Lord if he seemed incompetent or lacking in the skills needed to lead. That's why when the Highland Lord dies, and his son, if he has a son, or someone from a family with the next strongest claim, declares himself the Highland Lord, he must first pass the Three Tests – of skill, courage and knowledge."

Thomas' mind drifted back a few years to a time when he sat through much the same lesson. Rynlin and Rya had brought him to the Circle, knowing it was time for him to join the Sylvan Warriors. Of course, as was their wont, they had forgotten to mention that he would have to pass three challenges before he could assume his place among the Sylvana. Why did everything always involve threes?

"For the Test of Skill," continued the gray-haired, craggy-faced warrior, "the candidate must fight the Marcher most skilled in the sword and the Marcher most skilled in the spear. He must defeat his opponents without killing them, but the champions must fight to kill.

"For the Test of Courage, the candidate must enter the Ravine, a slit between two of the largest mountains in the Highlands that hides unknown dangers. The candidate must retrieve from the Ravine the crown worn by the Highland Lord, a silver circlet that every

Highland Lord has worn. Remarkably, when a Highland Lord dies, the crown disappears and returns to its place in the Ravine, awaiting the next Lord of the Highlands. I was there when it happened with Talyn, actually. As soon as he breathed his last in the Hall of the Highland Lord, the crown vanished."

Coban broke himself out of his reverie, scratching at his bushy mustache.

"For the Test of Knowledge, the candidate must answer questions put to him by the eldest leader of the Highlands that confirm the candidate's knowledge of the Highlands and its people. But, even if the claimant passes all the Tests, he still is not officially the Lord of the Highlands. No, we like to make things really difficult," Coban laughed.

"Any Marcher can then challenge the claimant to mortal combat. Now, admittedly lad, a challenge is a rare thing, happening only a handful of times in the last thousand years. It's always a possibility, but truly, if a claimant can pass the Tests, he has earned his place as the Highland Lord, and we recognize that. If a challenge is made, the claimant must defeat the challenger. If he does, he is proclaimed the Highland Lord. If, however, the challenger wins, that person gains the right to take the Three Tests. The process then begins all over again."

Thomas listened carefully to Coban's explanation of the steps to be followed, matching what the former Swordmaster said to his lessons with Rynlin on the Isle of Mist. He smiled at the complexity of it all, but he saw the structure in the process. There was a simplicity to it that seemed to go unnoticed.

The Highlanders wanted the best possible leader for their Kingdom. The Tests and other requirements ensured that's what they got, and history had borne that out. Though many Kingdoms had suffered through inept, unqualified rulers because they had a higher regard for birth rather than merit, the Highlands had never faced such a problem. They couldn't afford it, considering their small population and the greed of the other Kingdoms.

Thomas acknowledged what he must do. He could hear his grandfather in his head, repeating the words from the glade: "It is time, Thomas. It is time to stand on high."

And he knew within his heart that the spirit of his grandfather spoke the truth. Thomas could feel it now. The fear and indecision had disappeared, replaced with a new purpose and confidence. He was meant to be the Highland Lord, to follow in his grandfather's footsteps. More important, he was meant to free his people and make the Highlands strong once more.

Coming to that conclusion seemed to lift a weight off his chest, freeing him from what he had seen as the burden of having to return to the Highlands. He had been wrong all along. Yes, what he must do in the Highlands was an additional responsibility, yet by accepting it, by broadening his perspective and seeing it not just as a duty, but as an opportunity, Thomas gained a new appreciation for his position in life.

"And if the candidate passes the Three Tests and survives a challenge, what happens next?"

"He becomes the Highland Lord," replied Coban, looking at Thomas curiously.

"I'm sorry, Coban. That was a poor question. What I meant to ask was, do the people of the Highlands accept the candidate as their Lord?"

"That's a strange question, Thomas."

"Indeed it is, Coban. But you see my point, don't you? As you said, if the person seeking the throne passes the Tests and any challenge, then by right he becomes the Highland Lord. But the power and strength of the Highland Lord comes not from some declaration like, 'I'm now the Highland Lord, so you've got to do what I say.'"

Thomas laughed softly. "I've been away for quite some time, Coban, but I know that's not how Highlanders look at things. No, they treat people with respect when those people have earned their respect. A perfect example is the saying that you'll never see a Marcher on bent knee unless he's making a wedding pledge to his sweetheart.

"To succeed as the Highland Lord now, with all the challenges we face, the people of the Highlands must accept the Highland Lord not because of his passing some ritual or standard, but because they believe in him and what he can do for them. They must see hope and a future that replaces the shackles of slavery so many Highlanders have experienced during the past decade with the freedom we are so accustomed to. They must believe that through the Highland Lord they will be strong once more."

Coban reminded himself to breathe, losing himself for a moment in Thomas' words. Briefly, his mind jumped back to when Talyn Kestrel was still alive. Life had been like that back then, and it wasn't so long ago, was it? Only ten years.

"If he has a legitimate claim, passes the Tests, and survives any challenge, they do."

Coban leaned back in his chair, his eyes still filled with visions of the past.

"You know, Thomas, this is what we need. We need a new Highland Lord. It's the only way we'll survive. Then we could drive out the reivers and the warlocks and reclaim what was ours. Then we could go after the bastards who did this to us."

Thomas smiled viciously at the thought of doing just that. Highlanders were known for many things – courage, strength, fortitude, and a long memory. No slight or crime ever went unpunished, no matter how long it took for retribution.

"But we don't have anyone to lead us, certainly not anyone worthy of the title Lord of the Highlands. Now most of the chiefs are concerned primarily with protecting their villages and herds from the reivers and warlocks. And they've been doing that for so long that many have forgotten just how strong we used to be when all the villages gathered for war, when all the Marchers waited at the border for the latest invasion of some treasure-grubbing monarch. But that ended when Talyn Kestrel and his son, Benlorin, were murdered."

Mention of his father sent a shiver down Thomas' spine. His father had blamed Thomas for the death of his mother, Marya, and would have nothing to do with him as a baby or child. As a result, the job of raising him had fallen to his grandfather. After a while, when Thomas was old enough to realize what was going on, and Talyn could no longer fool him into thinking that his father was too busy protecting the northern border of the Highlands to spend time with him, Thomas no longer held any feeling for his father, allowing his resentment and bitterness to grow.

In fact, when Talyn told him that Benlorin had been murdered right before he escaped from the Crag, Thomas had experienced absolutely nothing when told the news. Yet, now a feeling of sadness crept over him. Why? Thomas shook it off. He didn't have time to waste dredging up memories and reopening old wounds.

"But there was a grandson," said Thomas.

"Yes, there were stories of the boy surviving," sighed Coban. "Although I didn't spend much time with him, you remind me of him a bit. It's strange, though. Even after all that time, rumors of the Lost Kestrel still circulate through the Highlands. The last time he was seen alive, he was about to enter the tunnels beneath the Crag, and that was almost ten years ago. If it was more than a myth then, I doubt it is anything but that now. Whoever murdered Talyn Kestrel — and I'm quite certain who was ultimately responsible — most likely hunted the boy down as well."

"I remember that night so well," Coban continued. "Soon after we entered the Hall of the Highland Lord through Talyn's study, the Ogren began pounding on the doors, their massive blows slowly cracking the oak beams. We fought like demons, but it wasn't enough. Though we held the beasts for a time, we couldn't stand against them forever. And through it all, Talyn Kestrel was at the front of our wedge."

Tears of pride appeared in Thomas' eyes. He had never before learned what had happened during the rest of that terrible night.

"With every swing of his sword a reiver or Ogren fell dead at his feet. And, truly, it looked like we might be able to hold against the onslaught." Coban's face darkened. "But then the warlocks appeared and we had no defense against their Dark Magic. A bolt of energy struck Talyn in the chest, killing him instantly."

Coban pounded his fists together angrily. "Worst of all, there was nothing we could do about it. Nothing!" Coban fell back in his chair in frustration.

"We fought our way free and went in search of the boy, following his route beneath the Crag and then through the forests surrounding the monolith. The whole time we had to avoid reiver search parties, which gave us an added sense of urgency. With Talyn and Benlorin dead, we knew the grandson was our only hope. We tracked the boy all the way to a glade in the southeastern Highlands, but from there we found no sign of him. We searched for days, but nothing. It was the strangest thing. He couldn't have just disappeared. There had to be some explanation, some tracks, but there was nothing. We had no choice but to assume the worst."

Thomas had never known that Marchers had come looking for him. What if Coban had found him instead of Rynlin and Rya? How would his world have been different? He forced those interesting but distracting questions from his mind. As before, he didn't have time for such things.

"It sounds like you did all that could be expected of you, Coban."

"I know, I know," the Swordmaster said, sighing heavily. "Many a Highlander has said much the same. But you see, Thomas, that single event has brought us to where we are now. If the boy had lived, would our homeland be free now? Would we have suffered through all the indignities and pain? Killeran has served as Rodric's regent in the Highlands for almost ten years. We might not recognize him as the regent, but the rulers of the other Kingdoms do.

"At the next Council of the Kingdoms, the ten-year period ends, and then Rodric will be able to take the Highlands for his own and do what he wants with us. Fighting the reivers now is considered war. Once that ten-year period ends, and Rodric assumes control, it's considered rebellion. And most of the rulers of the other Kingdoms have a dim view of rebellion. It makes them decidedly uncomfortable."

"Yes, there was a time when the High King was simply a figurehead, whose sole purpose was to maintain order at the Council," continued Coban. "But Rodric has been trying to change that ever since he became the King of Armagh. I think he fancies himself as the second coming of Ollav Fola, the greatest High King ever to hold the title. Some rulers, like Gregory of Fal Carrach and Sarelle of Benewyn, are smart enough to see it. Others simply choose not to.

"They'll certainly get a rude awakening when Rodric turns his attention on them. The man's as slippery as a snake and as devious as a fox, and he'll do whatever's necessary to achieve his goals. He's not satisfied as the King of Armagh. He wants more. And if he truly wants to become the next Ollav Fola, taking control of the Highlands is certainly a good first step."

"Then perhaps it is time for the Highlands to take its rightful place among the Kingdoms," said Thomas, sitting on the edge of his chair, his eyes burning a bright green. "What if I said that there was something we could do to stop Rodric? What if I said we could make the Highlands strong once more?"

"I'd call you a fool and a dreamer," snorted Coban, chuckling softly, his bushy white mustache revealing his teeth.

Thomas' intensity silenced Coban in a matter of seconds.

"You're serious?" Coban asked incredulously. "You're really serious?"

Thomas reached down to the floor, grabbing hold of his scabbard. He pulled the blade free, allowing the bright steel to capture what little light there was in the room. To Coban, it was as if the sun had burst through the clouds on a gray, murky day. Thomas held the blade in front of him so that the Swordmaster could get a better look.

Coban examined it for a moment, the puzzlement clear on his face. It appeared much like any other blade. But then he noticed the markings where the blade met the hilt, and the meaning of the sword dawned on him. He never thought he would see this particular blade again.

"The Lost Kestrel is not a myth," said Thomas, trying to judge how Coban would react.

The Swordmaster seemed to be a bit wild-eyed, and Thomas had no way of guessing what he would do when the truth of what he was about to say registered with the old Highlander.

"In fact, he's not even lost."

Coban recognized the blade. He had seen it hundreds of times at the hip or in the hands of his friend Talyn Kestrel. The last time he had laid eyes on it, Talyn had given it to his grandson, and Thomas had taken it into the tunnels as— Coban shot up from his chair, stumbling backward as one of the curved legs of the rocking chair caught his feet.

"The Sword of the Highlands!" exclaimed Coban, his eyes glued to the steel. His eyes latched onto Thomas' with a feverish intensity. "Are you—"

He was having a hard time giving words to his thoughts with his mind in such a jumble.

"Are you the one?"

Coban failed to keep the growing excitement from his voice. After all these years, could it really be happening? Would he finally have a chance to atone for what had happened? Would his people finally have the hope they craved so desperately?

"Are you truly the Lost Kestrel?"

Thomas sat quietly for a moment, staring at Coban. This is it, he thought. His response now would forever change his life. Would he be able to maintain control of the events about to unfold? Or, as seemed to happen most of the time, would he simply be drawn along by the tide, performing those duties and obligations

119

required of him, whether he wanted to or not? Thomas pushed those thoughts from his mind. He would control his life, not some prophecy. It was his choice now to return to the Highlands and assume the mantle once held by his grandfather.

Thomas saw the hope rising within Coban and the fire in his eyes that had been missing for such a long time. He remembered the ghostly expressions of the Highlanders Killeran forced to work in the mines. He had taken away their freedom, their reason for living. They had been no more than the walking dead, waiting for their turn to step across to the other side.

As soon as Thomas and Oso had freed them from the cages and shown them that if they fought back against the reivers and the warlocks they could win, in seconds the light had returned to their eyes. Though weak, sick, and tired, they had struggled through an incredible ordeal to attain their freedom, in essence to regain their lives. If he could do that for all the Highlanders who had suffered during the past decade, then it would be his greatest and most important accomplishment.

Thomas rose from his chair, sliding the Sword of the Highlands back into its scabbard. He then removed the leather guard on his right wrist, revealing the birthmark his grandfather had warned him to never show to anyone for fear it would lead to his death.

Coban stared at the mark, the raptor's claw. It was unmistakable and undeniable. His eyes bulged in recognition. It was almost too much for Coban to take, yet Thomas' words drew him back, sending through his body a rush of adrenaline that made him feel twenty years younger.

"I am Thomas Kestrel, son of Benlorin, grandson of Talyn. It is time for the Highlands to have a Lord once more."

Thomas' words struck Coban like a physical blow, forcing him to drop back into his chair. Strangely, words he thought he would never remember returned to him, running through his mind of their own volition. They were uttered two decades before by Thomas' mother, Marya, as she held Thomas soon after she gave birth to him, and right before she died: "You will give men hope, victory, if you remain true to yourself. You will be a man above all others."

Looking over at this young but determined Kestrel, Coban promised himself that he would from that moment forward devote himself to ensuring that her prophecy became a reality. For if it did, the Highlands would be free once more.

CHAPTER TWENTY-SIX

THE CALL

"What do you think they're talking about?" asked Oso, pacing in front of Coban's cottage, his brow furrowed and hands clasped behind his back. "Thomas has been in there for more than an hour."

"I'm sure you'll find out soon enough. Why don't you sit down? You're tiring me out."

Having just returned from her errand, Anara sat cross-legged in the grass to the side of the cottage and out of Oso's way, calmly whittling away on a piece of wood. The pretty Highland girl had let her short auburn hair grow longer since escaping from the Black Hole, blossoming into ringlets that kept dropping down into her eyes.

Oso now found her almost irresistible, but he still wasn't ready to admit it. That was all right with Anara. She had a great deal of patience, and as time passed it simply allowed her more chances to close the jaws of her trap. Though that was a crude analogy, she knew, it was right on point.

In fact, she was enjoying herself quite a bit. Oso kept glancing at her, wondering what the secret smile on her face meant. She could almost laugh out loud at his lack of understanding, but she knew that was to be expected of most men. By the time Oso realized what was going on, he'd have absolutely no opportunity or idea how to escape, and that suited her just fine.

"But what could be taking them so long? You should have seen the look on Thomas' face when he arrived. It was the same expression he wore when we burned down Killeran's fort. There was a sharpness to his features, his eyes, that was scary."

Oso stopped his pacing for a moment right in front of the cottage door. He watched Anara as she worked the piece of wood slowly into the shape of a bear. He marveled at her skill. It was remarkable, really, what she could do with her hands. For her, a piece of wood was much like an artist's canvas. She could create virtually anything. She was so much more skilled with her hands than he was.

A spear or a sword in his hand felt like an extension of his arm, but for anything else that required dexterity, he was all thumbs. Oso was about to continue his pacing when much to his surprise the door of the cottage slammed open and Coban burst out, running straight into him and sending them both sprawling to the hard-packed dirt.

"Blast it, Oso! What are you doing standing right there?" Coban regained his feet in a matter of seconds, while Oso remained on the ground trying to recapture the breath that Coban had knocked from his lungs. "No matter. There's no time for that now. No time at all."

Coban grabbed Oso's hands and pulled him back to his feet.

"Aric!" he shouted, surveying the village. "Aric!"

"What's going on, Coban?" Oso asked in a forced whisper, now bent over and still searching for a deep breath. A concerned Anara was at his side now, her hand resting comfortably on his back.

Several villagers gathered around Coban's house in a loose semicircle, wondering the same thing as Oso. Not even news of an approaching raiding party got Coban so excited. In fact, no one could recall Coban ever being so excited. Finally, a tall Highlander with curly black hair arrived.

"What's the matter, Coban? Reivers?"

"Get your bagpipes and go up to the knoll, Aric," commanded Coban, taking on the voice of the Swordmaster, a voice that everyone in Raven's Peak knew quite well. "I'm calling a council at the Pinnacle in three days' time."

"A council, Coban?" asked Aric, somewhat surprised. "But we had one just a few months ago. Why—"

"Do it, Aric!" commanded Coban. "Do it now!"

Recognizing the grim look on Coban's face, Aric set off at a run in search of his bagpipes.

"Coban, what's going on?" asked Oso, having regained his voice and breath. "I haven't seen you this excited since we routed that band of reivers a few weeks ago."

The crowd around Coban's cottage had grown larger with more than a hundred Highlanders waiting expectantly. They were all curious as to what was going on.

Coban reached back, grabbing hold of Thomas' right arm and pulling him out of the doorway, where he had waited in the shadows, not really comfortable with all the attention. He resigned himself to it, though. There was no going back now, and it was only going to get worse.

"This is why I'm excited," said Coban, looking at Thomas expectantly.

Thomas saw the hope burning fiercely in Coban's eyes and even more so the desire for freedom. This would be the first step on that path. Thomas silently hoped that he would be able to complete the journey.

Stepping forward so all could see, Thomas pulled his sword from his scabbard and held it above his head, allowing the sun to shine brightly on the blade. Many of the Highlanders gazed at the sword with puzzled looks. Those expressions slowly changed as understanding began to dawn on them.

Thomas drove the tip of the sword into the dirt, allowing it to stand up straight. They could see it now. It was unmistakable. The raptor's claw etched into the steel. That could mean only one thing. The Sword of the Highlands. But what of the boy? Thomas then removed his wrist guard, allowing everyone to see the mark on his arm. The raptor's claw again. The mark of the Kestrels. The mark of the Highland Lords.

Like everyone else, understanding was slow to dawn on Oso. But as he saw the sword and the mark on Thomas' forearm, everything seemed to come together. He had even given the sword back to Thomas while they escaped from the Black Hole, but he hadn't looked at the blade closely then, as he was focused on other things. Oso had been too young to have ever seen the raptor's claw before, but he remembered it vividly from his lessons.

The story of the fall of the Crag came back to him in a rush. It was rumored a traitor had allowed the reivers and Ogren into the Crag, for that was truly the only way they could have destroyed that almost impregnable fortress. Talyn Kestrel had died during the battle, Benlorin Kestrel soon before that, but no one knew what happened to the grandson. To Thomas Kestrel!

Now it was all truly coming together. Many believed the grandson had survived, leading to the legends that proliferated throughout the Highlands and had grown in their telling as each year passed. Oso had never given the rumors much thought, but the mark and the sword told him to believe, while his entire being begged him to believe.

"The Lost Kestrel," he whispered.

Anara had grabbed his hand, and she now squeezed it hard as she too came to grips with a legend come to life.

Thomas smiled. "I was lost, Oso. But no more. I am home."

In the distance, the sharp notes of the bagpipes began their lonely trail through the Highlands, echoing off the mountains and carrying for miles around. Soon other bagpipes would play, carrying the message even farther to every village in the Highlands, calling the village chieftains to the Pinnacle.

For Coban and the others, the notes drifting on the air held even more importance as they continued to stare at the young man in front of them. For them it signaled a new time for the Highlands, one of rebirth.

Thomas examined all the faces staring at him, studying their expressions. Many appeared to be awestruck, others skeptical, but all wanting to believe, all wanting the fear and despair that had become a common part of their existence to disappear, all wanting to replace it with hope – and freedom.

Thomas understood that. But more important, he knew it was the beginning of a long journey. And the first step would be proving his worth. He was not the Lord of the Highlands yet. Not until he passed the Tests.

CHAPTER TWENTY-SEVEN

THE FIRST STEP

K aylie stomped through one of the many gardens hidden throughout the Rock, kicking at the gravel path in frustration and sending the small stones into the flowerbeds. Learning how to fight with a sword was easy compared to this. She sat down heavily on a bench situated against the back wall of the garden, taking a moment to collect her thoughts.

Why was this so difficult? She just couldn't understand it. Thomas had shown her twice how to lose herself in nature, yet she couldn't succeed without his assistance. A pang of guilt struck her, but she quickly pushed it from her mind – or at least tried to. Kael was right, of course. She had made a mistake, and no matter how horrible that mistake may have been, she needed to move on and live her life. Though actually doing so was much easier said than done.

Thomas had described the Talent to her in depth, and she had been both terrified and fascinated to learn that this remarkable skill simmered within her. Unfortunately, she knew of no one who could teach her, and mentioning it to anyone could lead to some uncomfortable circumstances. Many people believed the Talent was a myth, others that it had died out long ago. As a result, anyone with any skill in the Talent was often branded a user of Dark Magic, a power that came from the Shadow Lord.

So those who did have a knack for the Talent often didn't use it, and by not using it the skill eventually diminished to the point where it was no longer usable or simply disappeared. Kaylie had kept her secret these past few months, unwilling to be branded a witch, yet she also didn't want to lose her skill. It was too exciting, too exhilarating, to give up. And, in fact, developing her skill in the Talent could prove to be extremely useful when she assumed the throne of Fal Carrach.

It was almost time to make her way to the practice yard for her daily session with Kael, but she decided to try her hand at the Talent one more time. Concentrating on the brackenberry bushes lining the far wall of the garden, she tried to push her awareness into the foliage. Sweat began to form on her brow as she strained for some contact.

About to give up, she remembered Thomas suggesting just a gentle nudge rather than trying to slam through a brick wall. Suddenly she felt a strange sense of recognition. Finches, chatterboxes and jays filled the bushes, and she could pick out each one distinctly.

Her excitement at finally achieving success almost led to a break in her tenuous connection, so she redoubled her efforts to prevent losing it. Much to her surprise, this time it was much easier to gain control of the Talent, and her added efforts expanded her senses beyond the bushes and the wall. Remarkable! It seemed that once you accomplished something with the Talent, it became easier to do a second time. And even easier the third and so on, until a particular skill became second nature.

She extended her senses farther beyond the wall, traveling slowly down a rarely used corridor in the Rock. She stopped when she came upon two people talking, and though she was on the other side of a wall and a good distance away, she could still hear their words quite clearly. The guilt that it was impolite to spy on someone's conversation quickly passed through her, but the topic of the discussion immediately quashed the thought.

"As I said, everything is ready," said a raspy voice.

"And the girl? What of her?"

The second voice was stronger and held a note of authority.

"She will be taken care of," the raspy voice replied. Kaylie could almost imagine the person grinning at the words. "I suggest you worry about your part in this business. We must move quickly. If Gregory discovers our plans—"

A bolt of fear shot through Kaylie. What could they be planning? And how would it affect her father? She strained for every word, not realizing in her excitement that it wasn't necessary since she still held a strong grip on the Talent.

"We must all take risks. Besides, he knows nothing, and it will stay that way. Until, of course, the arrow pierces his heart, but by then it will be too late."

"When will our helper be arriving?" asked the raspy voiced.

"Tonight. At the Blue Moon Inn down by the harbor."

"How will I recognize him?"

"By the scar on his neck. Also, he will be wearing..."

Kaylie jumped up in alarm. They were moving beyond the range of her ability in the Talent! She tried desperately to extend her senses once more, but this time her efforts led to a complete loss of her control and the Talent slipped away from her. Cursing her luck, she quickly grabbed hold of it once again, pushing it beyond the wall and as far down the corridor as she could, but the two men were gone. Blast it!

Overcome by the physical effort required in controlling the Talent, she dropped to the gravel path as a wave of exhaustion swept through her. She stayed there for several minutes trying to regain her senses. She didn't realize how much of her energy she had poured into this single and simple use of the Talent.

It was a good lesson for her. As she sat on the gravel path, her mind ran in a hundred different directions, attempting to piece together what she had overheard. The two men planned to assassinate her father. And the girl they were talking about was her. What was she supposed to do?

CHAPTER TWENTY-EIGHT

RENEWED ENERGY

The excitement of the previous day had infused the people of Raven's Peak with a sense of urgency and determination. All the men of fighting age, some former Marchers and others having just reached their maturity, prepared for the journey to the Pinnacle. Thomas and Oso sat in Coban's two rocking chairs as they watched the Swordmaster gather his things. They were leaving within the hour. They had to reach the Pinnacle by late afternoon tomorrow, and it was a day's trip to the east.

Satisfied that he hadn't forgotten anything, Coban cinched his bag and turned to his two companions. Thomas could see there was something on his mind by the twist of his brow.

"What's bothering you, Coban? There's no point in trying to hide it."

"So in addition to everything Oso has told me about you, you can read minds also?"

"No, I can't do that," replied Thomas. "And I'm not sure I'd want to if I could. But it's fairly obvious that something is gnawing at you. What is it?"

Coban sighed. "I mean no disrespect, Thomas, but I must ask you something."

"Go ahead, Coban. I'd rather have everything out in the open."

"Why wait until now to announce yourself?" the Swordmaster asked, obviously uncomfortable with the question, but still feeling the need to ask it.

His joy at Thomas' announcement had not yet dissipated, but the rational part of his mind wondered why the Lost Kestrel had waited almost 10 years to reveal himself.

"Why not after you destroyed Killeran's fort? Why not before that?"

Oso sat back in his chair, not expecting the question. Tension filled the room. He had wondered the same thing the day before, but chose not to broach the subject. The fact that Thomas declared himself at all was enough for him.

Thomas stared at Coban for what seemed like an eternity, yet was only a few seconds. His expressionless face revealed nothing. He had been expecting this question, but he still didn't know the best way to answer it. Finally, he decided to simply tell the truth.

"When I was escaping from the Crag, my grandfather gave me three charges. One of those charges was to remember, to remember that I was a Highlander, a Kestrel Highlander. I knew that one day I had to return, but truthfully, I wasn't sure I wanted to."

"Why not?" asked Oso, finding the idea preposterous. Why not want to return to your home?

"Because when I was growing up in the Crag, I wasn't treated very well. Almost everyone thought my mother was a witch, and because I was different, they thought I was one too. Only my grandfather treated me well. Everyone else simply tolerated me because I was the Highland Lord's grandson."

Coban bowed his head in shame. "Thomas speaks the truth, Oso. He was treated like a stranger in his own home. I'm sorry, Thomas. I should have done more to help you."

"Please, Coban. There's no reason to apologize. What's done is done. I spent the next ten years with my grandparents, and it wasn't until a few years ago that I learned how Killeran and his reivers were exploiting the Highlands. So I tried to help as best as I could. I had considered announcing myself, many times in fact, and I almost did after burning down the Black Hole. I was certain that you would recognize me when we first met, Coban. But you didn't, so I chose to keep the secret awhile longer."

"Why?" asked Oso, still puzzled.

"Because it didn't seem like the right time. I just didn't feel ready. I knew that if I declared myself then, I would have failed. I truly believe that."

Thomas pushed himself out of the chair and began pacing around the small cottage, trying to bring some order to his thoughts.

"My grandfather said I would know when the right time would be, but the years kept going by, and I was well aware of the approaching deadline for validating my claim."

"Then what did it?" asked Coban.

"About six months ago I made the mistake of trusting someone I shouldn't have. I was captured by

Rodric during the Eastern Festival in Tinnakilly. He accused me of being a murderer. Since none of the other rulers was strong enough to oppose him, he put me in the Labyrinth."

"The Labyrinth!" exclaimed Coban. "No one has ever escaped the Labyrinth."

Thomas smiled. "That's no longer true. I got past the traps and killed the Makreen. As you probably know, according to the law I should have gone free. But Rodric concocted another story and more false allegations. He tortured me. He enjoyed that quite a bit, in fact."

Thomas' smile grew larger – and more menacing, his grin appearing almost feral.

"He paid for it though. I escaped. And that's when I knew. I was lying in a small glade at the edge of Oakwood Forest when the spirit of my grandfather visited me."

Coban sat down heavily. This was almost too much for him to take in.

"Talyn?"

"Yes, Coban. Talyn's spirit visited me. I can't tell you how, but that's what happened. He told me it was time. And after I recovered from my injuries, I knew it as well. It was time to come home."

Thomas stopped pacing and fixed both men with a steely gaze. "I'm sure many others will also wonder why I waited so long, and they'll have little patience for my explanation. All I can say is that I will do my very best. I will free the Highlands or die trying."

Thomas' words energized Coban, lighting the fire in his eyes once more. He could see his old friend in his grandson. Yes, Thomas was different in many ways, but some of his characteristics and traits were unmistakably those of his grandfather. Hidden away in this quiet young man was a charisma that could very well sweep up an entire Kingdom.

"As will I," said Coban, offering his hand to Thomas, who gladly took it. "I was your grandfather's man, Thomas. As you probably remember, his Swordmaster. I will do whatever you need me to do. I'm your man now."

"Thank you." Thomas smiled. He always knew that he could count on Coban. "Then come with me, Swordmaster, for we have much to do."

CHAPTER TWENTY-NINE

SIGNS

"You can see the signs," said Catal Huyuk, bending over the rocky path leading around the mountainside. "It's faint, but the signs are still there. Ogren, Fearhounds, in numbers we haven't seen for several hundred years."

The tall warrior stood up. There were few trackers better than Catal Huyuk, and none had the ability to follow movements across stone as he did.

"It's as we feared," said Rynlin, scanning the surrounding cliffs for any movement.

You could never be too careful in the Charnel Mountains. Since the Shadow Lord had taken up residence in the heart of these peaks, their nature had changed. Once they had rivaled the Highlands in their beauty and majesty, but no more. The Dark Magic of the Shadow Lord had altered the landscape, blackening the peaks and turning the soil into a gritty, pitch-black substance.

These mountains were dead. Perhaps the most unnerving aspect of them was the silence. Birds and animals no longer lived here, only the creatures of the

Shadow Lord – and they preferred the night. Of course, there was also the wind. Sometimes you could hear voices within it. Calling to you. Teasing you. Seducing you. If you weren't vigilant, they could consume you.

"Yes, something is going on," said Rya. "But what?"

Rya and Rynlin had scouted the mountains for the past week, looking for some evidence that the Shadow Lord prepared to march south across the Northern Steppes with his Dark Horde. By all indications he wasn't ready for that yet. There were no signs of larger groups or base camps. What worried them, though, was the telltale evidence that something was afoot — signs such as the one Catal Huyuk had just picked out, smaller groups of dark creatures, all edging closer to the southern border of these dark peaks.

"A smaller force, perhaps?" suggested Catal Huyuk. "Clearly, based on what we've found, Blackheart is not yet ready to march against the Breaker. But perhaps he has some other goal in mind. There is much going on in the Kingdoms at the moment, and I wouldn't be surprised if he attempted to influence certain events."

A screech farther up the peak startled the three companions, Catal Huyuk drawing his axe from his belt and Rya and Rynlin both taking hold of the Talent. Just as quickly, silence reigned in the Charnel Mountains once more. The three studied the surrounding area carefully, looking for any activity. Satisfied there was none, they relaxed somewhat, though Catal Huyuk still held his axe and Rya and Rynlin retained their grip on the Talent. Most likely some dark creature had succeeded in finding an early meal.

"I think you're right, Catal," answered Rynlin. "We suspect the Shadow Lord is allied to the High King. With the Council of the Kingdoms approaching, it stands to reason that they have some plan in mind. And it may involve Thomas."

"I knew I should have gone with him," fretted Rya, her thoughts turning to her grandson.

"We discussed this, Rya. He has to do this on his own."

"I know, Rynlin," answered Rya, sighing in frustration. She wanted so desperately to be watching over her grandson. But she knew she couldn't. Rynlin was right. He had to do it on his own. Still, that wouldn't keep her from worrying about him.

"He will succeed," interjected Catal Huyuk. "He is a strong boy. And there is a power in him that I have never seen in anyone else. Worry if you want, Rya, but it's unnecessary. He is a Sylvan Warrior, and rightly so. Soon he will be the Highland Lord, and again rightly so."

Catal Huyuk spoke as if his words were simple logic, as if there were no other possibilities.

Rya smiled at the fearsome warrior's confidence. "Thank you, my friend. I hope you're right."

"There is no hope in this, Rya," replied Catal Huyuk. "I am right."

Rynlin tried not to laugh during the exchange. Once Catal Huyuk made up his mind about something, there was absolutely no way to change it.

"Are you still planning on leaving us, Rya?"

"Yes," she replied. "I'm curious about what happened yesterday. As you know, I don't like leaving questions in my wake, especially when they're connected to Thomas, even if just indirectly."

"All right," said Rynlin. "Catal Huyuk and I will continue our scouting and swing a little farther south. We'll try to find where the Shadow Lord's creatures plan to make their appearance on the Northern Steppes. Perhaps there's something we can do to dissuade them."

"Just be careful, Rynlin. Don't take any unnecessary chances." Rya's tone was one that brooked no argument.

"Rya, do I ever?" Rynlin's innocent expression looked completely out of place.

"Yes, you do. And especially when you're with Catal. You two make a dangerous pair."

"You injure me with your words, my love," said Rynlin, adopting a melodramatic pose. "To have so little faith in me, what am I to do?"

The diminutive woman struck her husband in the chest with her fist, catching him off guard.

"Just remember what I said, Rynlin. If you do anything stupid, I'll skin you alive."

Then in a flash of white light she was gone. A large eagle stood in her place. The bird squawked one more warning then lifted off the ground, using its powerful wings to pull itself higher into the sky as it headed south.

"A remarkable woman, your wife," said Catal Huyuk, watching the eagle become no more than a speck in the distance.

"Yes, she is," said Rynlin, rubbing the spot where his wife had hit him. "Remarkable, and dangerous."

"An intriguing combination," said the tall warrior. "Perhaps one day I will find a woman like that."

"If you do, my friend," said Rynlin, grabbing his traveling pack and heading farther up the small trail, "run for the hills. You won't know what you've gotten yourself into until it's too late."

CHAPTER THIRTY

KNOWING THE WAYS

"As I was saying the day before yesterday," said Coban, "Once you pass the three Tests, you may have to face a final challenge."

Thomas smiled as he followed Coban along the hunter's trail. Winding around the base of the mountain the path eventually led to the Pinnacle. Behind him were Oso, Aric and the other Highlanders from Raven's Peak – almost two hundred men in all. Most wore their cloaks tight around their shoulders, protecting against a damp misty rain. The day had dawned cloudy and cold, and had only gotten worse.

Thomas knew exactly what he must do to become the Highland Lord, but he chose to humor Coban. Obviously, the Swordmaster was nervous, as he rarely rambled on like this. Better to let him get it out now. With Coban's explanation and Rynlin's before that regarding the requirement that must be met to "stand on high," the Highland phrase for becoming the Lord of the Highlands, Thomas wasn't too concerned about what was going to happen during the next few days. He was certain the Tests would be challenging, but he doubted they would be as difficult as the obstacles he faced when seeking to become a Sylvan Warrior.

Instead, Thomas concentrated on what he would have to do after becoming the Highland Lord. Several critical issues demanded immediate attention, and probably a few others he wasn't aware of. He had to remove the reivers once and for all. True, he and Oso had dealt them a serious blow with Rynlin and Rya's help during their escape from the Black Hole, but that wasn't enough. The reivers still controlled much of the lowlands. He would have to root them out.

He also had to do something about the dark creatures terrorizing the northern Highlands. If he allowed them to gain a foothold, it would prove even more difficult to expel them than the reivers. And, of course, the sands in the hourglass were running dangerously low. In six months the rulers of the Kingdoms would gather at Eamhain Mhacha for the biennial Council of the Kingdoms. If he failed to make a claim for the Highlands, his homeland would revert to Rodric's control. And that was something he simply refused to allow.

He had returned the wrist guard to its place, covering the birthmark that signified that he was the blood of Talyn Kestrel, the last Highland Lord. He had done it partly out of habit and partly out of practicality. Traveling the Highlands, even in the higher passes, was still a dangerous proposition because of the reivers and dark creatures. Better to be prepared so he could nock an arrow to his bow if there was a need. At least that's what he told himself. He didn't want to admit that after almost ten years of hiding his identity, he still wasn't comfortable acknowledging his true heritage.

Maybe these immediate crises were actually opportunities, Thomas considered. He knew how some of the Highlanders would react to his claim, even with the proof he carried in his scabbard and on his forearm. Some would be skeptical. Others would accept him immediately. A few would probably oppose him. He would need to act quickly to consolidate his support, and the best way to do that was to give his people a purpose.

In cruder terms, by getting them to do something, they wouldn't have the time or the inclination to think. Then, before they realized it, the Highlanders would have gotten used to their new Highland Lord, and he with them he hoped.

"Thomas. Thomas, are you paying attention?"

Coban stopped suddenly, about to take another hunter's trail that branched off the one they were on. This one still wound around the mountain, but the steeper path offered faster access to the top of the mountain.

"Yes, Coban," Thomas lied, not wanting to upset the Swordmaster. "I was just trying to take in everything you were telling me."

"Good," replied Coban, satisfied by Thomas' response. He started up the new trail with his men following after. "Just let me do the talking when we get there. Stay in the background."

Thomas nodded. Coban had explained how Highland politics had evolved in the absence of the Highland Lord and the constant threat of attack and enslavement by the reivers. Each village chief had become a power in his own right, much like a lord in any of the other Kingdoms. The chief was responsible for the safety of the people living in his village.

Though some combined their forces when an attack from the reivers was imminent, that wasn't always a practical defense because of the isolation of some of the villages. And it was these villages that Killeran preferred to prey on. So the village chief had grown in power, becoming accustomed to it, and of these, Renn, Seneca and Nestor were the strongest. If Thomas could win these three over, then many of the other chiefs would follow.

Then there was Shagan. Coban had actually grimaced when saying his name, as if it left a bad taste in his mouth. He was almost as powerful as the other three chiefs, but Coban held out little hope that Shagan would support Thomas.

"And don't forget to stay away from Shagan," said Coban, making Thomas think the Swordmaster had read his mind. "He is the only other Highlander who has a claim for ruling the Highlands, but it is so slight, the only way for him to actually become the Highland Lord is to challenge a more worthy opponent. Then he would finally gain the right to take the Tests himself. I actually thought Shagan might challenge your grandfather after he had passed the Tests, but he didn't. Shagan's a smart one. I guess he valued his life more than risking it on a warrior's luck. And that was the only way he would have won if he challenged Talyn – luck.

"Yet even after Talyn stood on high, Shagan was a problem. It's been eating away at him ever since. Everyone knew he wanted your grandfather's place, but there was no way he could get it. So watch out for him, Thomas. You can expect a challenge from that one. Or something worse, like a knife in your back. As the years have passed, his bitterness has increased."

"Don't worry about that, Thomas," offered Oso, pulling even with his friend as they continued their march up the steep trail. "He'll have to go through me first."

"Don't let Anara hear you say that," joked Thomas. "If she finds out you're picking fights, Shagan will be the least of your worries."

Several of the Highlanders following after chuckled, overhearing the comment.

"I can handle Anara," boasted Oso, though he kept his eyes on the ground.

He didn't want his friend to see the red in his cheeks. In his heart he knew the truth of it, he just wasn't ready to admit it to himself yet.

"Of course you can, Oso. Of course you can."

Thomas and the Highlanders continued the remainder of their journey in silence, each man lost in his own thoughts, though they all paid close attention to the surrounding forest. The marks of passage were obvious, as many Highlanders had reached the gathering place before them, but still better to be safe.

Finally, after another hour's travel, they reached the plateau, which stretched across the top of the mountain for more than a mile. At its far end, towering cliffs rose up, dwarfing everything else in sight. Thomas used his sharp eyesight to pick out a jagged cut in the heights, what he assumed to be the Ravine. Thomas stared at the cliffs for some time, wondering if he would succeed in his quest to become the Highland Lord. There was only one way to find out, of course.

The sounds of laughter and shouting drew Thomas' attention away from the cliffs. Looking out across the plateau, he saw that several thousand Highlanders had arrived before them, each separate camp representing a different Highland village. Thomas realized that Coban had scheduled their arrival for this time on purpose. With the sun about to set, it was almost three days since Thomas had revealed his true identity to the people of Raven's Peak. As the Highlander who had called this gathering, Coban was required to be the last to arrive.

"The other chiefs know we are here," said Coban, glancing at Thomas. "We do not have to do anything until tomorrow morning if you like. Perhaps you could use the time to prepare for—"

"Thank you, Coban, but that won't be necessary." Thomas gripped his friend's shoulder in acknowledgement. "I have waited too long already. Let's begin. These people deserve to be free."

Pride surged within Coban as images of Talyn crept into his mind. The similarities between grandfather and grandson were remarkable. If Thomas was but half the man Talyn had been, then the Highlands would once again be free. Coban knew that for a certainty. And if Thomas was more than that? If he proved to be even more than Talyn, then the other Kingdoms need worry, for there were several reckonings due.

Coban nodded and started out across the plateau. Thomas walked beside him with Oso leading the men of Raven's Peak. As they passed each encampment, Coban greeted the chief, but he never stayed longer than a few seconds. Ignoring the questioning gazes at the suddenness and timing of this council, Coban marched steadily toward the center of the plateau, his face a serious mask. Thomas studied the chiefs and other Highlanders as they passed by, recognizing the three chiefs Coban had mentioned.

"A council so soon, Coban? This must be serious business indeed," said a large Highlander with a grey beard that ran halfway down his chest who sidled up next to the Swordmaster.

Shagan. Coban's description was a good one. Shagan was bald, even lacking eyebrows. The fires that swept through the Crag had been the cause, and the hair had never grown back. His most distinguishing characteristic, however, was the other result of the fires – the left side of his face had been horribly burned. Now it was a ridged mass of scar tissue, hidden only in part by his beard.

"Have you finally found a wife? Am I right?" the tall Highlander asked maliciously. "That's got to be the reason."

Shagan laughed deeply.

"Only you don't know what to do with her so you've come here for advice." Shagan's laugh became a bellow.

Several of the Raven's Peak Highlanders had their hands on the hilts of their swords. Aric's blade was halfway out of the scabbard until Oso pushed it back down. A good man, Oso, thought Thomas. Now was not the time to start a feud. There was too much at stake. Though Coban's eyes burned brightly with anger, he understood that as well. He ignored Shagan's insult and continued across the plateau.

Shagan dropped away from him, not wanting to waste any more of his time if he couldn't get a rise out of the old Swordmaster. He glanced briefly at Thomas. Who was that boy? he wondered. He had the look of a Highlander, but then again, he didn't. Strange indeed. There was something about the boy that stoked his memory, but nothing rose to the surface.

"Ah, well, perhaps a bottle of wine would help," murmured Shagan, before sauntering off to his tent.

With his final destination in sight, Coban increased his pace. The Pinnacle rose before them. Constructed of several large slabs of stone that rose twenty feet into the air, the platform allowed all who gathered around it to see and hear who spoke. Coban walked up the steps to the top, Thomas right behind him. Oso and the Raven's Peak men stopped at the base. Once at the top, Coban breathed deeply, trying to calm his already jangled nerves. The time had come.

CHAPTER THIRTY-ONE

MYTH MADE REAL

T ime passed with agonizing slowness, though it was only a few minutes. Normally, when a council was called, it began on the morning after the third day since the summons. But not this time. Coban stood atop the Pinnacle as still as a statue, his eyes taking in all the Highlanders who had gathered. And there he waited as the chiefs of the various villages realized what was going on and then made their way toward the Pinnacle, their men following in their wake.

All the while Thomas stood silently besides Coban, realizing that he broke with tradition, for only one person was supposed to stand atop the Pinnacle at a time. He could see it in the faces of some of the Highlanders, wondering who this boy was and by what right he stood with Coban. Who was he to ignore the traditions of the Highlanders?

Thomas noted to himself that traditions, no matter how important they may be in the eyes of those who held true to them, often hindered change. And that was something his people would have to adjust to quickly. Change. If they were to succeed in regaining control of their homeland, they would have to adapt to new circumstances.

Finally, Coban moved, if only barely. He turned in a slow circle, seeing that thousands of the Highlanders who had gathered on this cloudy day had surrounded the Pinnacle, waiting for Coban to begin. Now, finally, after all these years, he could set in motion the process for redeeming himself and assuaging the guilt he still struggled with over Talyn's death. Now he could finally exact his own revenge on those who had ransacked his homeland. Now he could do his part to make the Highlands strong once more.

And with those thoughts, he looked at Thomas. There was a question in Coban's eyes, wondering if the young man was ready, for from this point forward he was no longer a boy. He couldn't afford to be. Thomas nodded, his expression serious, his eyes intense.

Coban stepped forward to the edge of the Pinnacle. He studied the crowd of Highlanders. Normally, they milled about and talked quietly as they waited for a speaker to start. But not this day. No, there was an anticipation in the air, an energy. Everyone sensed it.

"My friends, I never thought I would live to see this day," began Coban, sweeping his eyes over the crowd as his words easily carried across the plateau for all to hear. "We have suffered greatly since the murder of Talyn Kestrel, yet we have survived."

Many of the Highlanders nodded in agreement, their faces grim. Everyone in the crowd recalled the atrocities inflicted upon them – the loss of a loved one to the reivers or the mines, the destruction of their homes, the pillaging of their beloved mountains – and the frustration and impotence they felt at not being able to prevent it from happening.

"Through it all we have stood strong," said Coban. "Though small in number, we have fought against the reivers and their warlocks. We have fought against the dark creatures sent across the Northern Steppes. We have refused to surrender our homeland to a cowardly High King. Our homes have been burned, our loved ones murdered or worked to death, yet we continue to fight, for we are Highlanders, Marchers to the core, and to do anything else would be a betrayal of all that we hold dear."

Coban's words immediately swept up the Highlanders, taking them hurtling to the very roots of their existence. Thomas was shocked by the skill with which the old Swordmaster had begun his speech. Coban, indeed, was a surprising man. For the first time in a decade, the Highlanders remembered who they were – and all that was taken from them. Their anger and frustration had risen to the surface. All they needed now was an outlet.

"Almost ten years ago a traitor allowed reivers and Ogren to destroy the Crag, and with the destruction of our ancient fortress we lost our Highland Lord, Talyn Kestrel," said the Swordmaster. "Perhaps the greatest of the Highland Lords, in fact, for he ruled the Highlands fairly, taking note of the interests of each Highlander and the greater good of all, always balancing the two to ensure the Highlands remained strong."

Several Highlanders shouted their agreement, many too young to remember Talyn Kestrel, yet recalling the stories told by their elders around the cook fires.

"Since his death the Highlands have been desecrated by the High King's raiding parties, by the Dark Magic of his warlocks, by the very presence of the Shadow Lord's creatures!"

Shouts of anger erupted from the crowd. Coban had caught them in his trap, and he wasn't about to let go. His voice softened, becoming almost a whisper.

"My friends, those days are over."

Absolute silence greeted his words. Coban looked out upon the hopeful faces staring up at him for a moment, letting the anticipation build.

"For years we have heard whispers of the Lost Kestrel. For years we have hoped for his return. My friends, I must admit, I truly didn't believe in the Lost Kestrel. I was at the Crag when it fell, I searched for the boy when hope was lost, and he was never found. Though I truly didn't believe in the Lost Kestrel, hidden away in my heart the hope of his return lingered."

Many of the onlooking Highlanders nodded their agreement. Like Coban, they didn't believe in the Lost Kestrel, but a small part of them desperately hoped that they were wrong. The anticipation continued to build. Many of the Highlanders stepped forward, moving closer to the Pinnacle. Coban had reignited their hopes and dreams by stoking their anger. Now was the time to give them what they wanted.

"My friends," said Coban, almost whispering, though his words still carried easily across the plateau. "The Lost Kestrel is not a myth. The Lost Kestrel has been found. The Lost Kestrel stands before you!"

Shouts of surprise and exclamation erupted from the crowd, but Thomas ignored them. He stepped past Coban and drew his blade. And at the very same time he pulled the steel free from the scabbard across his back, the misty rain stopped and the sun broke through the clouds that had draped the Highlands for most of the day. Holding the blade above his head, he allowed the sunlight to play across the steel. Then, as he had done in Raven's Peak, he thrust the tip of the sword into the rock of the Pinnacle so it stood on its own.

The crowd grew quiet. They knew the blade. They were mesmerized by it. They saw the etchings. Whispers in the crowd carried backward so that all could hear, even those in the back. "The Sword of the Highlands!" "Truly, the Sword of the Highlands!" There was no other blade like it, having been passed from father to son, and in this case grandfather to grandson, for millennia.

Then the crowd finally turned their eyes to Thomas, who stood there calmly. He removed his wrist guard, and with a tantalizing slowness, rolled up the shirtsleeve of his right arm. With the birthmark now visible, he thrust his arm into the sky.

At that very moment the sun burst through the clouds in all its glory, centering its rays on the Pinnacle and the young man standing there. The light illuminated Thomas in an almost blinding aura, reflecting off the stone polished over the centuries by the tread of Highland boots. They gazed at the mark on his arm. They recognized the claw. They were mesmerized by the mark of the Kestrels.

Shock registered on the faces of most of the Highlanders. Like Coban, most had never truly believed they would see this day. None truly believed they would ever gain their freedom. None truly believed they would regain their homeland. But no more. They believed now. The myth had come to life. Many of the older Highlanders saluted, recalling their days as Marchers, but most simply stared dumbstruck at this boy who looked like a Highlander but didn't, completely unprepared for what had just happened.

"I ask to take the Tests," said Thomas strongly. "I ask to prove my worth so that I may take the place of my grandfather as the Highland Lord."

Shouts of joy and cheers greeted his words, the tremendous noise echoing off the surrounding peaks and drifting on the wind to the farthest reaches of the Highlands. Thomas felt tremendous relief, but he understood that he had only just begun along a difficult and dangerous road. Yet he didn't feel fear; only resolve. These were his people, and he would do all that was necessary to return them to the glory they deserved.

In the morning, the Tests would begin, and the future of the Highlands would ride on his shoulders.

CHAPTER THIRTY-TWO

MENTORS

Kaylie sat on her four-poster bed, deep in thought, twirling several locks of her raven-black hair between her fingers. Night fell upon the land, the shadows stretching from ceiling to floor and the sounds of the evening making their way through her windows. With the sounds came the chill of the breeze, and though the cool air brought goosebumps to her arms, she barely noticed.

What was she supposed to do? Call in the guards? If she did, it would serve little purpose. She couldn't identify the assassin or his accomplices. Calling out to the guards would most likely alert the assassins that their plot had been discovered. They would simply wait until all the activity died down, and then they would take action. No, she couldn't allow that to happen.

She had spent the last few hours searching for a solution, but nothing had come to mind. After overhearing the conversation that turned out to be an assassination plot, she had immediately gone in search of her father, only to discover that he had left on one of his journeys.

Gregory of Fal Carrach was known for many things, such as his fierce loyalty and his strict adherence to the law. But what truly endeared him to his people was his desire to improve their lives. Unlike some other rulers, he did not view his power as a way to advance his own interests at the expense of his people. Rather, he saw it as a responsibility to do as much as he could for those who lived under his rule.

So every few months he made a circuit of his kingdom, getting a feel for what was going on, making sure that all of his subjects, even those located in the hinterlands of Fal Carrach, knew that he was interested in their lives and their well-being. It also gave him the chance to check on the preparedness of his border troops, which was a constant concern because of Loris of Dunmoor's frequent raids and the rumblings coming from Eamhain Mhacha.

Kaylie suspected, though, that there was another reason. Her father chafed at some of the duties forced upon him as king. He hated having to deal with trade emissaries, though he understood the need, and he absolutely detested courtiers. He could do without their constant flattery and false smiles. So his journeys around the kingdom gave him a chance to escape from his more loathsome duties. She truly couldn't blame him. If she were in his position, she'd do much the same.

She glanced at the paintings she had had moved into her bedroom just a few months before. There were three, all on the wall facing her bed so she could see them every morning as soon as she woke up. She had promised herself after the mistake she had made with

Thomas that she would never repeat it. She would become an excellent queen in the tradition of the Highlands – a fighter and a diplomat. So she had searched through the history of Fal Carrach for women who could serve as her inspiration.

On the right was the portrait of Moira of the Black Feathers. Born of peasant stock, she had married a lesser noble of Fal Carrach – Kaylie couldn't remember his name — who lived near the western border. The lord was killed defending his home from a Dunmoorian raid, and Moira had sworn revenge. She taught herself how to fight.

Once she had deemed herself worthy she had challenged the Dunmoorian lord who had murdered her husband to a duel. The arrogant bastard had laughed at her, but then decided to have some sport. She killed him in a matter of seconds. She then did the same to every man who had participated in the raid. And why the name Black Feathers? Upon the death of each man, she had dropped a black feather on his chest — the feather of a crow, an animal associated with the dead.

The other two women were quite different in that they had never, at least to Kaylie's knowledge, picked up a sword, but they were every bit as strong as Moira of the Black Feathers. In the center was a portrait of Faethe Loraliee, daughter of Tomasin, King of Fal Carrach a thousand years before her father. Betrothed to a young lord named Vitalis, she had been devastated to learn that he had disappeared after a bloody battle against dark creatures near the Charnel Mountains.

Yet she still hoped for his return as his body was never recovered. Despite the many suitors, she refused their advances. Several years passed, and most everyone called her a fool for holding out hope for her loved one's return, so her father demanded that she pick a husband. Right before she was supposed to make her choice, her love returned, having been sold into slavery after the battle. It had taken him years to escape, but Faethe's steadfastness had won out.

And then there was Elenea, wife of Boranon, who was in fact a lesser-known king of Fal Carrach. But perhaps that was because it was Elenea who truly reigned in Fal Carrach while her husband sat the throne. Boranon lacked most of the skills required of a king, but Elenea more than made up for it, functioning as the power behind the throne. During her time, she expanded Fal Carrach's borders to what they are now.

Kaylie examined each of the portraits closely. These strong women had taken matters into their own hands. As she gazed at their pictures, she finally realized what she needed to do. She'd simply have to take care of things herself.

CHAPTER THIRTY-THREE

TAKING A RISK

K aylie crouched in the small, shadowy alcove, waiting patiently for the cooks to leave. The scullery maids were almost done cleaning the pots and pans, and as soon as they finished, the cooks would bank the fires and close the kitchens until four in the morning, when the first shift arrived to bake the day's bread.

With the kitchen empty, Kaylie could sneak out the delivery entrance and mingle unobtrusively with the people going across the bridge into the town of Ballinasloe. It was late evening, and she hoped she wouldn't miss the rendezvous, but she had little choice. This was the only way to leave the Rock unnoticed.

She had chosen carefully from her wardrobe to ensure a good disguise. She wore a black cloak over a dark green riding dress, something that a fairly well-to-do merchant would own. Also, she had twisted her long black tresses into a bun, something that she rarely did.

Upon checking her appearance in the mirror before making her way to the kitchen, she had been quite pleased with the effect. No one would recognize her except her closest friends or those people she came into contact with frequently at the Rock. And she doubted that she would meet any of them where she was going.

Suddenly, the kitchen was plunged into darkness, and she realized the scullery maids had finished their work and the cooks were leaving. She waited five minutes then made her way to the delivery entrance. Opening the door quietly, she peeked outside. The occasional lamp hanging from a long pole offered some light. No one was about. She quickly exited the kitchen and walked towards the entrance used by the servants who lived in Ballinasloe.

She was in luck. Several women were leaving for their homes. Kaylie quickened her pace until she was right behind the group, though not actually a part of it. As she followed them out onto the bridge her heart skipped a beat as the soldiers glanced in her direction, but much to her relief they nodded a good evening and returned to their watch.

Once across the bridge, she stopped in a small sandwich shop to ask directions. She discovered that the Blue Moon Inn was only three streets to the west looking out onto the bay. In most cities walking alone by the docks at night meant you would be either robbed or murdered, or both. For a woman, there was another danger, one that Kaylie didn't want to think about. But such was not the case in Ballinasloe. Her father kept a close eye on those who preyed on the citizens of his Kingdom by maintaining a diligent City Watch. In fact, on every street corner, several members of the Watch stood at their posts.

After only a few minutes' walk, Kaylie reached her destination. She stood in front of a well-kept inn, a shingle with a moon painted a deep blue announcing to all who passed by the name of the building. Kaylie took a deep breath and then stepped quickly up the stairs and through the open doors, steeling herself for what she would have to do.

She was alone. She was frightened. But she had never felt so alive.

CHAPTER THIRTY-FOUR

UNWANTED ATTENTION

Kaylie sat uncomfortably at the end of the wooden bench. She had waited for three hours, dragging out the dinner she had ordered for as long as possible. And then she had simply sipped at her wine, refusing more than a second glass. She needed to keep her senses about her. She shifted her weight for the hundredth time. No matter how she moved it felt like a splinter stuck her in the worst possible place. Sighing in frustration and boredom, she took another sip from her glass.

The innkeeper certainly didn't mind the slow speed with which she drank. She had paid him twice the cost of the meal and enough silver for ten drinks so that she would be left alone by the serving staff. But there was nothing she could do about some of the others enjoying a night's respite in the inn.

"Hello, darling," said a tall man, a shaggy mustache drooping over his upper lip.

He wore the clothes of a noble and had obviously grown the mustache to hide his youth. Probably no older than Kaylie, he was obviously trolling the inns and bars for a good time.

"Perhaps you'd allow me the pleasure of buying you a drink?"

"No, thank you," Kaylie replied sternly, hoping the tone of her voice would put him off.

But it was not to be. He pulled a chair closer to her then sat down, his knee grazing hers under the table.

"Just a drink, milady, and no more. Truly I only want to enjoy the company of a beautiful woman such as yourself."

Kaylie was absolutely certain she knew what the lord meant by the word company.

"I said no, milord. Now please leave me be. The friends I am waiting for would not look on it kindly to see you here now."

The young lord ignored her warning.

"Milady, rarely does a young woman like yourself choose not to drink with me." He reached under the table and grabbed her knee, bringing a burst of red to her cheeks. "You may not realize who you speak with. I am Kenesil, a Lord of Benewyn. Obviously you are a merchant. My father and I run one of the largest trading conglomerates in the east. If you satisfy my desires, I'm sure there is some arrangement we can reach to advance your—"

The young lord's words ended in a strangled gasp. He looked down to see the point of a dagger pressed into his groin.

"Milord, as I said, leave me be." Kaylie's voice was stone cold, her face an angry red. "And if you do not satisfy my desires, well, with the flick of my wrist you won't be satisfying anyone's desires ever again."

The young lord gulped, looking down at the dagger poised between his legs one more time.

"My pardon, milady. My pardon." In an instant he was up from his chair and out the door.

Kaylie replaced the dagger in the sheath on her belt. Five men had tried to work their magic upon her during the evening, and of the five the last was the most difficult to persuade that she wasn't interested. She smiled to herself. The look of fear on that young lord's face was worth the aggravation he had caused her. Kaylie shook her head in frustration. It was well past midnight and time to leave the Blue Moon Inn. Much to her dismay, she realized she must have arrived too late for the meeting.

To her surprise a tall man with curly black hair walked in. More important, though his collar was pulled up high on his neck she could see the beginnings of a scar. The assassin! He stopped for a moment to survey the crowd. Then he moved quickly across the common room to join two men sitting at a table on the far side of the inn. The three immediately fell into conversation.

Though Kaylie tried to observe them surreptitiously, she couldn't get a good look at them. Remembering what she had done in the courtyard earlier in the day, Kaylie took hold of the Talent – something that was becoming easier and easier for her to do the more she tried it – and directed it at the three men.

"It will be done within the week," said the curly haired assassin, bent over the table so no one sitting nearby heard their whispers.

"How do you plan to do it?" asked the shorter man sitting at the table.

His companion looked to be much taller than he, but Kaylie could not see past the dark cloak that hid his body and face.

"That doesn't matter," replied the assassin contemptuously. "He'll be dead within the week and the Kingdom will be yours. That's all you need to care about. Understood?"

"But—"

The assassin cut off the shorter man's protest. "You have learned all you need to know. I have succeeded in this business for quite some time, as I'm sure you're aware. The reason for my success is that I tell the people I work for only what they need to know. I do not work for people who can't understand that restriction. Do I make myself clear?"

The taller of the two men simply sat there, seemingly uninterested in the discussion. The smaller man at first seemed to be insulted by the assassin's words, then nodded reluctantly.

"Yes," the shorter man replied sullenly.

"Good. Do you have the rest of my payment?"

The shorter man nodded again. "Here it is."

The assassin snatched it from him.

"Good. Within the week. Do not try to contact me again. If you do, I will have a second assassination to undertake this week. Do I make myself clear?"

The shorter man's face, though turned from Kaylie's prying eyes, appeared to change to a lighter shade.

"Yes. Within the week."

The assassin immediately rose and strode out of the inn. Kaylie considered following him, but decided against it. There was something about the man that frightened her. Besides, she had memorized his appearance. What she didn't know was what his two accomplices looked like. But Kaylie remained glued to her chair for a different reason.

Who would get the kingdom upon her father's murder? That was the question she needed to answer.

CHAPTER THIRTY-FIVE

RESCUE

Kaylie was still debating how to get closer to the two conspirators when they both got up from their table and headed for the door. Without thinking, she counted to five after they had exited and then followed. A small voice in the back of her head warned her that what she was doing was extremely dangerous. But the louder voice, which wanted to know who was trying to kill her father, drowned it out.

Stepping out into the night, she looked both ways down the street for the two men. Where could they be? They couldn't have disappeared so quickly. There! The bright moonlight not only reflected off the water of the bay, but off the bald head of the tall conspirator, something she didn't know while in the inn because he had kept the cowl of his cloak resting on the back of his scalp. The smaller of the two was talking animatedly, but the tall, bald man appeared to ignore him.

Kaylie counted five more seconds then started after them. The two men continued down the street for some time, which made Kaylie's task quite simple, especially because of the large number of people moving to and from the various bars and inns lining the road. And with the men of the City Watch appearing on every corner, she felt quite comfortable in her task. But then her prey turned off the main thoroughfare and began making their way through some of the back streets and alleys – places the City Watch rarely visited because most of Ballinasloe's citizens knew to stay away from them at night.

Despite her misgivings, Kaylie pushed on. She had little choice now but to follow more closely, otherwise she'd lose them going around a corner if she wasn't fast enough. Her strategy worked well for several minutes as she deftly stayed in the shadows. Yet the small voice in her head grew more insistent, warning her of danger. She ignored it, too focused on her task to pay any heed.

The two men turned right at the end of the alley and Kaylie hurried after, fearing she would lose them. Rounding the corner, she felt a rough hand take hold of her arm in a viselike grip, stopping her in her tracks. The sudden bulge of fear in her throat kept her from screaming.

"So what do we have here?"

Kaylie looked up at the two large men standing above her. The one holding her arm had asked the question. His grin showed several missing teeth.

"A spy I think," said the other hulking man. Just as tall as his friend, where the first had broad shoulders that belied his likely past as a brawler, the other carried most of his weight around his waist.

"Let me go!" demanded Kaylie. "You have no right to stop me. If you don't release me, I'll call for the City Watch."

Both men laughed at her threat, quite taken with the humor of it.

"Sorry girl," said the man whose belly threatened to explode out of his shirt. "The City Watch doesn't visit these streets very much. Scream all you want."

"What should we do with her, Lester?" asked the other bruiser. "Our boss won't like the idea of someone following him."

"Well, he didn't leave specific instructions, did he, Natul? He simply said to stop anyone who tried to follow after."

"We could throw her into the bay, perhaps? Tie a rock around her ankles?"

The one named Natul smiled gleefully at his idea, obviously quite pleased with it. Kaylie felt as if she were watching the whole exchange between the two brawlers from someone else's body. She couldn't believe they were talking so casually about murder. Try as she might, she couldn't break free of Natul's grip.

"Slitting her throat now would be the easiest thing," offered Lester, thinking deeply on the subject.

His employer really should have been more specific, he decided. He wasn't paid to think. He was paid to follow orders. Thinking made his head hurt.

Events were quickly getting out of hand, Kaylie decided. She reached for the dagger hidden in her belt, but before she could get it all the way out of the sheath, Natul's large palm engulfed her hand. He then pried the dagger from her fingers with relative ease.

"A feisty one."

"She is, Lester," said Natul. "She is indeed."

"You know, I like 'em feisty."

"Then perhaps we should teach her a lesson before we kill her," suggested Natul.

"Yes, a lesson," sneered Lester. "That's a good idea, Natul."

Kaylie shivered with fear. How could she have been so stupid? She should have guessed that whoever was trying to kill her father would take the necessary precautions to cover his tracks and ensure his identity remained a secret. She had been so focused on her task that she had ignored the warnings in her head.

She had to do something – and quickly! The leers of the two men set off her basic instinct for survival. She struggled as hard as she could to gain her freedom from Lester's grip, but her efforts were for naught. No matter how hard she pulled, it didn't affect him, nor did her frequent kicks at this legs and shins.

"A feisty one, indeed," laughed Natul, grabbing her other arm and helping Lester drag her toward the back of the alley. "This is going to be fun."

Kaylie screamed as loud as she could, but she knew that it was wasted effort. No one would hear her. And if they did, in this part of the city, no one in their right mind would venture out after a scream like that. Trying to gain control of her rapidly escalating fear, she reached for the Talent. But her terror got in the way, destroying any hope of concentrating. She couldn't believe this was happening. It couldn't! She was the Princess of Fal Carrach. How could she have been so foolish!

Lester and Natul had almost reached the end of the alley. Kaylie continued to struggle for a hold on the Talent. She had to succeed. She had to! Suddenly, a flash of white light burst around them, momentarily blinding her and her two attackers. Stunned by the strength of the flash, it took her a moment to realize that she was free of Lester and Natul, who were rolling on the ground in agony, their hands covering their damaged eyes. She felt a smaller hand grip her arm.

"Come with me, girl, if you want to live." It was a woman's voice, and the hand on her arm was helping her get up from the cobblestones. "Now, girl! We don't have much time."

With her vision still clouded by the flash of light, she allowed the woman to pull her down the alley and back out onto the street.

CHAPTER THIRTY-SIX

DARK VISITOR

S hagan let the empty wine flask fall to the soft grass beneath his tent, joining a half dozen others. The large Highlander scratched at the scar on the right side of his face, struggling to relieve an itch that never seemed to go away. At first, it had infuriated him. Now he was resigned to it, almost like a curse brought on by the fall of the Crag.

He grabbed another flask of wine from the small table set by his chair for that very purpose. Pulling out the cork, he took a swig, some of the liquid trickling down the side of his mouth and into his long beard, staining the grey whiskers red wherever the drops touched it.

For the thousandth time that evening he cursed his ill luck. He was in a foul mood, all because of that bastard boy. Talyn's grandson! How could he have survived the attack? He had been there. He had seen everything, heard all the stories from the other survivors. But never any mention of this boy. So he had assumed he was dead.

But now with the Sword of the Highlands in his hands and the Kestrel mark on his arm, that boy was about to proclaim himself the Highland Lord. In a moment of fury, Shagan threw the flask against the tent wall, then pounded the arms of his chair in frustration.

He had grown up with Talyn and had seen the many benefits given to the Highland Lord while his friend's father ruled the Kingdom. Gradually, Shagan's desire had become an obsession, until he would do almost anything to achieve his goal of becoming the Lord of the Highlands, or as he liked to translate it – to lord over the Highlands. But he had never had the chance to assume what he saw to be his rightful place among his people. His claim was too weak to ask to take the Tests. Nevertheless, perhaps he could still achieve his goal and the status he deserved.

After Talyn had passed the Tests, Shagan could have challenged him to a duel. If Shagan had won, he would have gained the right to take the Tests for himself. But he had chosen not to. He knew that if he had challenged Talyn, he would have died. There was no mercy in a challenge, not even between friends. So his anger and obsession had simmered over the decades, waiting for an outlet, yet knowing he had been stymied those many years before by his fear.

Yet now, with the appearance of this boy, his hope had been rekindled, only to be dashed once more. During the last few hours, he had heard the stories about the boy's fighting prowess, how he had killed the Makreen and Fearhounds and Ogren, how wolves and other animals fought for him.

If the boy was half the warrior he was said to be, Shagan realized that challenging the boy meant a certain death. He knew it with a cold certainty, much like he had decades before. Though he was quite a bit larger than the boy, he wasn't as strong or as fast as he used to be. Blast it! Some useless twig of a boy was going to take the Highlands away from him. His Highlands!

"You shouldn't drink so much before your great victory, Lord of the Highlands."

Shagan jumped up from his chair, flailing desperately for his dagger, the raspy voice sending a chill down his spine. He didn't succeed in grabbing his dagger until the fifth try, and only then when he looked it into his hand. He finally peered into the darkness, searching for the source of the voice, yet shadows greeted his eyes.

The laughter of his men entered the tent through a small slit in the back wall. Perhaps one of them had decided to have a little fun with him on this night. Well, once his head stopped pounding and his world stopped spinning, he'd find the jokester and make an example of him. Shagan sat down heavily in his chair once more, this time leaving the dagger within easy reach on the table. He didn't want to struggle with the task of having to put it back in its sheath.

"As I said," repeated the raspy voice, this time with a menace that chilled the air of the tent, "you should not drink so much the night before your great victory."

Without warning, a Shade stepped out of the darkness, standing right before Shagan. Seeing the ghoulish cast of the skin, the greasy dark hair and the milky white eyes, the large Highlander knew he couldn't be hallucinating. Shagan leapt back, or at least tried to through the wine-induced haze. Instead he stumbled out of his chair and knocked over the table. Seeing the dagger on the floor, he dove for it.

A hand shot out, catching him in mid-motion around his throat. The Shade held him in an iron grip, lifting him off the floor. Though the Shade appeared to be slight, he showed no effort or strain in dealing with Shagan's massive weight. It was much like a child holding a feather.

"You will listen to what I have to say," said the Shade, its milky white eyes showing no emotion, no feeling, nothing.

Shagan tried to nod, but realized he couldn't. He could barely breathe. He knew he didn't stand a chance if he attempted to fight. He'd be dead in an instant, and then his men would find his crumpled, withered body the next morning, the Shade having sucked out his soul for nourishment.

His terrifying fear gave him a sudden clarity, the effects of the wine disappearing for the moment. He would do anything the Shade wanted, anything to avoid that fate. Sensing his submission, the Shade released the Highlander, allowing him to stand on his own. Shagan gasped for breath, his hands going to his bruised throat.

"Decades ago you wanted to be the Highland Lord," began the Shade. "Now you want it again. But you don't have the skill to challenge the boy. I will help you."

Shagan almost laughed, then realized it would most likely mean his death.

"Why should I trust you?" he asked. "Ten years ago I did what your master wanted. Because of me you gained the Crag. But Killeran got the power. Not me, as had been promised. I've been living in a flea-infested hovel since then. Why should I trust you now?"

Shagan stepped back in fear, realizing he may have crossed over the line with his words. Yet the Shade stood there still as a statue.

"Do not ask questions," said the Shade, the creature's voice brooking no argument. "As I said before, your decision now will determine if you live or die. You do not have the skill to defeat the boy, but that doesn't matter. I will help you. During your duel, I will use my magic. You will—"

"You have Dark Magic?"

Shagan blurted out the question before he knew what he was doing, so intrigued he was by the statement. He had never heard of a Shade ever having skill in Dark Magic. Shagan's hands went back to his throat as he began gasping for air. It felt like a hand was squeezing his throat bit by bit, and it was getting harder and harder for him to breathe. Spots began to cloud his vision. The Shade remained where he was, not moving, its hands by its side. Suddenly, the pressure disappeared, and Shagan could breathe once more.

"Most don't, but my master has favored a few of us. Now back to my reason for being here. When the Kestrel passes the Tests, you will challenge him."

"Why not kill him with your magic now?"

Shagan's eyes bulged as he realized what he had done once more. He should never have drunk so much wine. He was going to die. He could see it now in the Shade's eyes. But for some reason the Shade relented.

"Because I need a distraction. You will be my distraction. If he suspects an attack with Dark Magic, he can defend against it. With you occupying his attention, before he realizes what I'm doing, it will be too late. After you kill him, you can do whatever you want, Lord of the Highlands. What is your answer?"

Shagan licked his lips in anticipation. Finally a way to achieve his goal, but at what price? Nothing was ever free, especially when it had to do with the Shadow Lord. But did it really matter? If he didn't agree, the Shade would kill him. He had no doubt about that.

Shagan nodded, and for the first time the Shade showed some emotion. The gaunt, skeletal creature smiled, revealing razor sharp teeth. The sight chilled Shagan to his very core, making him wonder if death now was preferable to what lay before him. Once you accepted a gift from the Shadow Lord, you were never free.

CHAPTER THIRTY-SEVEN

THE TESTS

"Are you sure you're ready, Thomas?" asked Oso, unable to keep the worry from his voice.

Oso had barely slept, his mind straying to what was to happen on this day, even though he would be no more than a spectator. Amazingly, his friend hadn't even stirred during the night.

Thomas grinned broadly, slapping his friend on the back as they navigated around the many tents and pavilions set up on the plateau.

"Relax, Oso. I'm ready."

"All right. All right. It's just that—"

"I know, Oso. I've been thinking about this moment for half my life, worrying about what would happen. Would I succeed? Would I fail? Would I live up to my grandfather's expectations? And now that it's finally here, I feel free. No matter the outcome, I'm doing what I should be doing. That's all that matters."

Thomas picked up the pace. He was a bit anxious, though he wouldn't admit it to his friend. Too much was riding on this for him to fail. So much, in fact, that he didn't want to think about it.

"Better for you to keep an eye on Shagan."

Oso nodded. "Don't worry, Thomas." His own worry disintegrated as his attention turned to this new task. "You can count on me."

"Of that I have no doubt," said Thomas.

They walked the rest of the way in silence, each consumed by his own thoughts. When they reached the last line of tents, they saw the other Highlanders already in place, standing in a loose circle around the Pinnacle. Oso slapped his friend on the back for good luck as they approached the throng.

As Thomas entered the crowd, it parted, giving him a path to walk through. Coban stood at the end, waiting at the foot of the Pinnacle. Oso followed Thomas through the crowd, stopping at the first row of Highlanders with the men of Raven's Peak. Oso made sure he had a clear view of Shagan.

Thomas continued past the crowd, which had left a wide circle open around the Pinnacle. Stopping a few feet in front of Coban, he nodded to his friend in greeting. Because Coban had been the Swordmaster for the last Highland Lord, he was responsible for officiating the Tests.

"Thomas Kestrel, grandson of Talyn Kestrel, the last Lord of the Highlands, asks to take the Tests," said Coban in a voice the carried to the very last row of Highlanders. "Will you allow it?"

The gathered Highlanders immediately murmured their assent, the request being nothing more than a traditional formality.

"So be it," said Coban. He then ascended to the top of the Pinnacle. "To become the Highland Lord you must pass three Tests: one of skill, one of courage and one of knowledge. We begin with the Test of Skill."

As Coban began the ceremony, Thomas allowed himself a moment to relax, probably the last moment he'd be able to relax for quite a long time. His eyes wandered the crowd, picking out a few familiar faces. For a moment, he thought he had seen the image of his grandfather in the crowd, but that wasn't possible. Was it?

A familiar voice spoke in his head: *It is time, Thomas. It is time for you to stand on high.* Thomas' eyes scanned the crowd, but the image of his grandfather didn't appear again. Talyn was here with him in spirit, somewhere, and that knowledge offered Thomas some comfort and relief.

"The candidate must defeat the Highlands' best swordsman and best spearman in single combat," said Coban. "Only then can we determine the candidate's true skill, for the Lord of the Highlands must be our greatest champion."

A buzz began in the crowd, the Highlanders' excitement difficult to contain as Renn and Seneca stepped forward, Renn holding a spear and Seneca a sword.

"The candidate must disarm both his opponents, but to kill them is to fail the Test. The swordsman and spearman must fight to the death, though they can grant the candidate mercy if the candidate so requests."

Thomas studied his opponents, seeing in both the confident demeanor and posture of veteran fighters, the best the Highlands had to offer obviously, or they

181

would not be standing across from him now. These men had fought in hundreds of skirmishes, fighting for a longer period of time than Thomas had been alive. To most people, such knowledge would have dispirited them. But not Thomas, knowing that his grandfather watched.

"The candidate may select any two weapons except the bow. What weapons do you choose?"

Thomas examined Renn and Seneca once more, appraising both much like his other grandfather, Rynlin, had done to him when they had first met. Finally, he made his choice.

"A quarterstaff."

"A quarterstaff?" Coban asked, not sure if he had heard correctly.

Many of the watching Highlanders gasped in surprise at the unorthodox choice.

"A quarterstaff," confirmed Thomas.

Coban nodded, though he didn't understand Thomas' decision.

"And your other weapon?"

"I don't need another weapon."

The gasps of surprise became cries of shock, and even Thomas' two opponents looked at him skeptically, wondering whether this boy meant to insult them by using just one weapon or he simply didn't know what he was doing.

They hoped he understood that fighting to the death meant exactly that. To not do so would dishonor both of them, and they couldn't allow that. Though Thomas may be the only hope for their people in escaping from the tyranny of the past decade, he would have to prove himself just like every other Highland Lord had since the Highlands gained its independence.

"You don't need a—" Coban stopped trying to figure out the logic of Thomas' decision and simply nodded his assent. "A quarterstaff."

A Highlander tasked with bringing the candidate his weapons stepped through the crowd and approached Thomas, carrying a finely carved quarterstaff made of ash. Thomas took a few seconds to get a feel for the weapon, pleased with its balance. Thomas nodded his approval.

"Then we begin," said Coban.

Renn and Seneca stepped forward, approaching Thomas with the grace demonstrated by the large cats that inhabited the Highlands. For them, there was no wasted movement. Every action had a purpose. They chuckled as they examined Thomas, who stood casually with his back to the Pinnacle, leaning on his quarterstaff for support. The boy didn't seem to have a care in the world. They'd certainly do their best to change his attitude.

As they closed on Thomas, Renn moved to his left and Seneca to his right. He had expected such a maneuver. The two Highlanders began circling him. Thomas moved away from the Pinnacle so that he'd have room and wouldn't get boxed in against the rock.

The tactic surprised Renn and Seneca, who thought Thomas would remain with his back to the Pinnacle to limit his opponents' avenue of attack. But Thomas knew that wasn't the way to win this fight. He had to end it quickly or he wouldn't stand a chance, thus his decision to fight on open ground so he could take advantage of his speed and agility.

He had chosen the quarterstaff as his only weapon for a number of reasons. First, he didn't want to kill either man, which was more difficult to do then with a sword or spear. As soon as he became Highland Lord he would need their support and help. Besides, the Highlands couldn't afford to lose any more men of their caliber. Too much was at stake.

Second, the quarterstaff was an excellent weapon against both the sword and spear. It matched a spear in its length and could be used in the same manner as a sword.

Third, he had already had some luck with a quarterstaff when dueling the Makreen – albeit with a slightly different type of quarterstaff, but nonetheless, why stop now?

Renn and Seneca watched Thomas carefully as he spun in a small circle to match the circle the two Highlanders wove around him, Thomas' quarterstaff spinning slowly in his hands, ready for the first attack. He didn't have long to wait. Renn jabbed with his spear and Thomas easily deflected the blow. Seneca followed right after with his sword, then Renn again and Seneca once more. Each time Thomas knocked away the lunge, knowing that they simply tested him, gauging the speed of his defense.

Believing that they had learned enough, Renn and Seneca began the main assault with both attacking at the same time from opposite sides. Thomas' quarterstaff was a whirl of motion as he defended himself, digging deep within himself for the resources needed to turn away the assault. The attack continued for several minutes, and many times Thomas escaped harm by only a hairsbreadth.

Renn succeeded in tearing a hole through one of Thomas' shirtsleeves while Seneca sliced Thomas' shirt across his belly, the blade coming frighteningly close to disemboweling him, but Thomas withstood the withering attack, his quarterstaff knocking away a lunge from Renn or both of his hands coming up on the staff to thwart a downward cut from Seneca.

Finally, it came to an end. Renn and Seneca stepped back, somewhat surprised that they had failed to draw blood. They expected Thomas to be as tired as they, but he simply stood there, quarterstaff held comfortably in his hands, breathing as if he had done nothing but stand there calmly for the past ten minutes.

While Thomas enjoyed the brief respite, noting that the activity had taken more out of his opponents than him, his mind worked furiously. There was absolute silence on the plateau, the gathered Highlanders captured by the spectacle unfolding before them. The only noise came from Renn and Seneca's breathing. Thomas had to make use of that advantage. He needed to end this before he got a spear or sword lodged in his gut.

Expecting Renn and Seneca to attack again at the same time, Thomas formulated his plan of action, mirroring it to the one he had used when fighting the shock troopers under the watchful eye of his grandfather. Then, he had almost won, but the third shock trooper had succeeded in getting past his defenses. Hopefully this time his plan would work with only two opponents.

Renn and Seneca approached once more, Renn again moving to his left and Seneca to his right. Thomas waited patiently, his quarterstaff twirling slowly through the air. He decided to take Seneca first. As both Highlanders attacked simultaneously, Thomas sidestepped Renn's lunge and knocked the spear aside. Thomas then lunged himself, but this time directly at Seneca, who at the same time was jabbing forward with his sword.

Thomas' attack caught the grizzled Highlander off-guard. Knocking the sword from Seneca's hand, Thomas struck the Highlander a hard blow in his gut with the butt of his quarterstaff. As Seneca buckled under the blow, Thomas reversed his staff and brought it down on the back of his head just hard enough to knock the man senseless.

Renn was shocked to see his friend fall so easily, and then he suddenly realized that the many rumors about this boy's fighting skills just might be true. He had thought that some of the stories had to be exaggerated. But it seemed that there was more than a kernel of truth to them. Locking away his worries, Renn waited for Thomas' attack. He was not to be disappointed. Thomas' assault came in a whirlwind of motion, his staff moving at a blinding speed as he searched for a whole in Renn's defenses.

The large Highlander struggled more and more, finding it harder and harder to match the speed of Thomas' attack. Thomas waited until he had the opening he wanted. Bringing his quarterstaff in low, he feinted a jab, then quickly brought his quarterstaff up, knocking Renn's spear from his hands. Before the Highlander could react, Thomas swung his weapon in a tight circle, taking Renn's legs out from under him. Renn landed heavily on his back, knocking the wind from him. He tried to rise but was greeted by the tip of Thomas' quarterstaff poised at his throat.

"Do you yield?" Thomas asked calmly, barely breathing hard despite the ferocity of his attack.

Renn croaked a yes and Thomas relented, moving the quarterstaff out of the way and allowing his opponent to roll over and recover. He then walked over to a groggy Seneca who was just regaining his senses. Thomas offered a hand to help the Highlander back to his feet.

The crowd had watched in silence, mesmerized by the duel, then suddenly realized that it was over. The Highlanders erupted with a tremendous roar. Thomas worried that Renn and Seneca would hold his victory over them against him, but he decided there was no point in worrying about something over which he had no control. They had done what was required, as had he.

CHAPTER THIRTY-EIGHT

TEST OF KNOWLEDGE

"Thomas Kestrel has passed the first Test," confirmed Coban. He then moved quickly to the next step. "Now comes the Test of Knowledge."

The crowd fell into a deathly quiet as an old Highlander stepped out onto what had been the field of battle. Nestor, his name meaning knowledge in the old tongue. Though his hair was completely white with a beard running down to his belt, his step was still light and his eyes held the gleam of youth. He was the oldest of the Highland warriors and could in fact be compared to the bards of old, for within him rested the history of the Highlands. Many of the books and documents that contained the Highland history had been destroyed when the Crag fell. For the past ten years, Nestor had done his best to write down what he and others remembered so that it wouldn't be lost.

He was about to complete his decade-long task, but the summons of the bagpipes had drawn him away. A bit put out by that, he wanted to end this quickly so he could return to finish his work. Then he could focus on recording what was to follow in the wake of this boy.

Though some Highlanders may still doubt the ability of this young Thomas Kestrel, Nestor did not. He saw the boy's passing the Tests as a given, but that didn't mean he would allow him to have an easy time of it during this Test. For, much like Renn and Seneca, doing so would bring dishonor to his name, and that was something no true Highlander would ever willingly allow.

"The Test of Knowledge consists of three questions," said Nestor, as much for the crowd's benefit as the candidate's.

Thomas groaned inwardly at the news. Why did everything always involve threes?

"First question. How was the first Highland Lord selected?"

Thomas stood as still as a statue for more than a minute, thinking back to his lessons with Rynlin and Rya. His grandparents had certainly prepared him well for this moment, and Thomas was actually glad now for the long hours of study they had required of him.

"Through a competition," answered Thomas. "Thousands of years ago all the Highland village chiefs gathered here at the Pinnacle. They then fought a series of duels, until finally one man emerged victorious, a chief named Yaren."

"And this Yaren then became the first Highland Lord. Correct?" interrupted Nestor, his eyes gleaming.

"No," answered Thomas.

A low murmur began in the crowd, again captured by the competition before them, this time testing mental acuity rather than physical. Many wondered at the wisdom of Thomas disagreeing with Nestor. They all

189

knew that no one could challenge him in his knowledge of the Highlands.

"He did not feel worthy. He said the man he defeated in the final duel, who had also bested all the other chiefs, was a better man and leader. Yaren was just a warrior. The other chiefs acceded to Yaren's wish and Cullen became the first Highland Lord."

Nestor examined the boy in front of him, secretly pleased by the response, though he maintained a façade of indifference.

"Correct," he said simply, immediately moving on. "Second question. For which ruler did a Highlander serving as a member of the honor guard give his life for the first time?"

"Queen Gueneva," Thomas responded instantly.

Nestor was somewhat taken aback by the speed of Thomas' response, his eyes widening a bit. Every Highlander knew the name of the first Marcher to die in service to another monarch – Sorin Strongbow – but for most the name of the monarch was a mystery. For centuries, Marchers had served as the personal bodyguards for almost all the rulers on the continent, until they had been betrayed. But Thomas did not allow himself to fall back into the story. He had one more question to worry about.

"Correct," said Nestor. "The final question. Ollav Fola, the first High King, was once asked this question. What is the greatest resource of the Highlands?"

Now it was Thomas' turn to smile. Nestor had asked a trick question, for the obvious answer was the wrong one. True, the Highlands held untold riches in the form of gold, silver, other precious metals and jewels, but that wasn't the most valuable resource found in the Highlands.

"The people," said Thomas.

The Highlands was not a populous kingdom. As a result, every Highlander mattered in the Kingdom's survival.

Nestor smiled. As he had expected, though he was a bit surprised by the celerity with which the boy had responded.

"Correct."

The old man stepped back into the crowd, which again erupted into a loud cheer that echoed off the surrounding peaks. Nestor had much to do. He would have to hurry with his history or he'd miss the changes he sensed Thomas brought with him.

Two down, one to go, thought Thomas.

Chapter Thirty-Nine

Test of Courage

"Thomas Kestrel has passed the second Test," declared Coban. "Now for the Test of Courage."

Coban pointed across the plateau where the cliffs rose up for several hundred feet. In the very middle was a small, jagged slit.

"Enter the Ravine and retrieve the crown of the Highlands."

Coban walked down from the Pinnacle and steered Thomas through the crowd of Highlanders, who opened a path for them. He then escorted Thomas across the plateau in silence, with the Highlanders waiting at the Pinnacle. As they reached the base of the cliffs, with the darkened Ravine right before them, Coban asked for Thomas' weapons.

The Test of Courage was one of inner strength. Weapons weren't needed or allowed. Thomas pulled the Sword of the Highlands from his back then began extricating daggers from shirtsleeves, boots and his belt. Coban was rather impressed by the cache of weapons Thomas hid on his body.

"Any idea what I can expect?" Thomas asked.

Rynlin and Rya had taught him about the first two Tests, but they were unable to offer much help on this, the last one.

"I wish I could," sighed Coban, as he gathered up all of Thomas' weapons. "The only people who know are those who have entered the Ravine, and the last to do so was your grandfather. Those who emerge never speak of it when they retrieve the crown. The others, those who aren't worthy, well, I'm sure you've heard about them."

Thomas had heard the stories, and that's what worried him. Those who had entered the Ravine, yet failed in retrieving the crown, usually never were seen again. Those few that did reappear, but had failed in their quest, were hopelessly insane. Whatever they had experienced in the Ravine had stolen their wits. Taking a deep breath, Thomas steeled himself, then walked through the gap in the stone.

After ten steps he was in complete darkness. He stopped for a moment, allowing his eyes to adjust. Thomas' eyes glowed a dark green, allowing him to see quite well in the darkness. Nevertheless, he had to watch his step. The footing was treacherous and the Ravine walls gradually closed in on him, forcing him to turn sideways in many places with his back and stomach squeezing against the stone walls.

He took his time as he traversed the narrow path, waiting for something to happen. Yet the darkness held only silence and stillness. Thomas stretched out his senses, searching for what waited for him ahead. But there was nothing.

Finally, after almost a half-hour of squeezing his way down the path, it began to open up, and with the larger space rays of sunlight started to illuminate the Ravine. Eventually the Ravine opened up to the point that a cart drawn by a team of oxen could easily travel along the trail Thomas now trod upon. Still, Thomas continued to take his time, waiting for whatever was supposed to happen next. The silence and stillness remained.

And then he saw it. He had reached the end the Ravine, and on top of a stone column carved by time sat the crown of the Highland Lord, a simple circlet made of silver.

Thomas approached cautiously. What Coban had explained was true. When the Highland Lord died, through some type of magic the crown disappeared and ended up here, waiting for the next Highland Lord to claim it. The last time he had seen the crown, his grandfather had worn it – the night the Ogren had sacked the Crag.

Memories came flooding back, but he pushed them aside. Now was not the time to reminisce. He extended his senses once more, this time searching for traps. But he found nothing. Slowly, he reached out for the crown. As his fingers brushed across the silver, he felt like he had been hit in the head with a sledgehammer.

All of the hopes, dreams, fears, worries and needs of the Highlanders, living and dead, rushed into him. In a sudden moment of clarity within the maelstrom that had taken over his mind, he came to understand the full weight of what it meant to serve as the Highland Lord. Yet, at the same time, the duties, the responsibilities, the burdens threatened to overwhelm him.

He felt his identity being pulled away from him, and he knew with an absolute certainty that if he let it go, he would exit the Ravine mad – if he exited at all. He'd never be able to find himself again within the whirlwind of emotions and feelings built up over millennia that tried to consume his very being.

Thomas struggled to gain control, to separate himself from the very consciousness of the Highlands. Slowly, slowly, as if he were unknotting tiny knots in a woven tapestry, he began to pull himself away from what threatened to overwhelm him. He was regaining a better hold on himself. Just when the thought he had finally regained control, a beautiful woman appeared before him, her dark chestnut hair pulled away from her sharp green eyes. There was a flicker of recognition in Thomas. Could it really be? No, it wasn't possible. It was almost too much for him to bear, his grasp slipping in the struggle to maintain his unique identity, the maelstrom of emotions and needs, hopes and dreams, fears and failures, churning faster, sensing victory.

"Do not let go, Thomas," said Marya Keldragan. He was too shocked to do more than stare at the spirit who stood before him. "You must stay strong, for the hopes of all, not just the Highlanders, rest on you."

With her words, it felt as if even more burdens had been thrown on Thomas' already sagging shoulders, forcing him to his knees. Marya reached out to her son, but there was a momentary flicker of annoyance in her eyes as she could do no more than that.

"Remember what I said, Thomas. When you were a babe you were marked. You can't escape it no matter how hard you try. You will give men hope, victory, if you remain true to yourself. You will be above all others. Remember that, Thomas. Remember."

And then just as suddenly as she had appeared, Marya was gone, replaced by another apparition, one Thomas had never expected to see, one he had no desire to see.

"You ruined my life, boy," said Benlorin Kestrel, his words seething with hate. "I would have gladly traded Marya's life for yours, but the choice was not mine."

The force of his father's words struck him like a physical blow, threatening to knock away the very last vestiges of his identity, even though Thomas thought he had steeled himself to his father's feelings years before.

"You will never live up to your forebears. The Highlands will fall, and it will be because of you," snarled Benlorin, his normally peaceful face twisted into one of rage. "You're not a pure Highlander, boy. You never will be. You'll never understand what it is to be a true Highlander. End this charade now, murderer, before you destroy my people."

Thomas dropped his hands to the ground, crawling into a ball, trying to withstand the terrible onslaught. He was losing himself. He could feel it. He was slipping away. Everything – the struggle, the pain, the loss — had been for naught.

"Enough!" The shout rocked the Ravine, sending stones flying from their perches along the sloped wall.

"You have no right to speak to your son in this manner."

The spirit of Talyn Kestrel stood before his son, hands on hips, his face red with rage.

"Pure Highlander he may not be, but he is a Highlander. He has the courage and strength to meet his responsibilities. He has shown it. He has lived it, despite every reason for him to forsake his past, to forsake the hold of a people that didn't want him. Did you meet your responsibilities?"

Talyn's words made Benlorin flinch.

"Thomas was not responsible for Marya's death, it simply happened. Yet you blamed your son, you blamed a babe! And I raised him because you shirked your duty."

Talyn drove his fist into his palm. Everything he had wanted to say to his son but never had when they were alive poured forth.

"You are the coward, Benlorin." Talyn lowered his voice to a whisper, though the words still bit sharply, as he intended. "Thomas has already proven to be more of a man than you ever were. You, Benlorin, you are the failure."

Unwilling to withstand the scathing attack, Benlorin's spirit disappeared. Yet, his stricken expression showed that Talyn's words had struck home. Through it all, Thomas lay on the ground, curled up into a ball, trying to maintain his sanity, trying to hold on to the very last bits of who he was.

"Thomas," Talyn's spirit called, reaching for his grandson as Marya had and also realizing that there was only so much he could do. "Thomas, fight it. You can win. You were meant to be the Highland Lord. You must be the Highland Lord. You can do this. You are stronger than us all."

His grandfather's encouraging words gave Thomas a renewed strength, allowing him to continue the struggle with the whirlwind of emotions playing through his mind. After several agonizing minutes, he realized he was winning, he was regaining control, until finally he locked away the consciousness of the Highlands in a separate part of his mind. He knew that from this point forward it would always be there with him, a reminder of his responsibilities, but it would never again threaten his sanity.

Slowly he rose to his feet, exhausted by his struggle. His grandfather stood on the other side of the column, looking down at the crown of the Highlands. "You have done well, Thomas. Very well. I always knew you would."

"Thank you, grandfather."

"Now it is time, Thomas. Take the circlet. You have met the charges I gave you. You are Thomas Kestrel, Lord of the Highlands. You must make the Kingdoms remember who we are. You must make them remember that we are strong, that we are resilient, that we do not forget those who injure us and those who help us. Take the circlet, Thomas. It is yours. You have made me proud to call you grandson."

With those final words, Talyn disappeared.

Thomas stared across the crown at empty space for a moment, hoping his grandfather would return, but knowing it was not to be. He turned his attention to the crown. Reaching down, his fingers closed around the silver circlet.

At the very same instant, he finally felt at peace with himself. He knew who he was now, what his responsibilities were, but unlike before when he saw his duties as burdens, he now saw them as a gift. He had been chosen for this task because there was no one better to assume it. The fate of the Highlands rested on his shoulders, and he accepted that responsibility humbly and willingly.

Turning from the column, he walked back through the Ravine. But this time, he did not have to squeeze past the walls. The magic of the place opened up the path so that it was wide enough for two carts. Thomas exited quickly, physically and mentally exhausted. He walked slowly across the plateau toward the ring of Highlanders, the silver circlet clutched tightly in his hand.

When they saw Thomas coming toward them, a huge roar erupted, shaking the very plateau upon which they stood. The Highlanders again made way for him as he strode slowly toward the Pinnacle, many inclining their heads, acknowledging Thomas for who he was. As he ascended the Pinnacle, the roar grew greater in intensity. Coban raised his hands for silence, and in an instant quiet once again reigned on the plateau.

"Thomas Kestrel has passed the Third Test," declared Coban, his voice ringing triumphantly. "If there is no one to challenge his claim, then—"

"I challenge his claim," said Shagan, stepping out from the crowd. Ripples of anger threaded their way through the Highlanders, but Shagan ignored it.

"I issue a challenge. The boy isn't fit to rule. Does this Lost Kestrel have the courage to accept the challenge?"

Coban sighed in frustration. He should have known the bastard would try something, but there was no way around it. If Thomas refused the challenge, his claim was forfeit.

"Do you accept the challenge?" Coban asked.

"I do," replied Thomas.

Though he stood atop the Pinnacle calmly, his eyes burned brightly with anger. Shagan may see him as only a boy, but he would soon discover that he was mistaken. Distinct from the first Test, now there would be no mercy shown during the challenge. No mercy at all.

"Then return here in one hour," said Coban. "The challenge will confirm if Thomas Kestrel is to be the next Highland Lord."

Chapter Forty

The Challenge

"Is what happens in the Ravine real, Coban?"

Thomas stood beside the Swordmaster at the steps of the Pinnacle, the Highlanders once again having gathered around for the challenge. Many of them, some former Marchers for his grandfather, had already come up to congratulate him.

Even Renn and Seneca, the two Highland chiefs he had defeated in the Tests, had offered him claps on the back and good wishes. For them there were no hard feelings. They had done their duty, as had Thomas. Though they knew it was a bit premature to offer congratulations — Thomas had to survive the challenge – it was clear that few if any of the Highlanders actually hoped that Shagan would succeed. But it was an important part of the making of a Highland Lord, so they abided by the traditions.

"I don't know, Thomas. I wish I did. Why? What happened in the Ravine?"

"I'd rather not say," Thomas replied quietly, the shock of meeting his mother, or at least her spirit, having worn off, but his father's words still haunted him.

Coban grunted that he understood. As he had explained to Thomas before he had taken the third Test, no Highland Lord had ever revealed what happened in the Ravine. And, honestly, Coban really didn't want to know.

A murmur rose in the crowd as Shagan pushed his way through, carrying a huge axe that was as long as a broadsword. His wicked grin made the scar on his face appear all the more gruesome.

"Time to die, boy," said Shagan, chuckling softly. "I hope you've enjoyed your life, because it's about to come to an end."

Thomas ignored Shagan, instead pulling his claymore free from the scabbard on his back. The last rays of the day's sunlight caught the steel, bathing Thomas in a golden glow. He looked into the crowd and locked eyes with Oso. His friend nodded.

They had spoken before the challenge. They both knew that despite Shagan's size, Thomas should win if he didn't make any mistakes. He was younger, faster and a better fighter. Yet they had both agreed that Shagan would not have made the challenge if he didn't think he could win. So Oso promised to keep his eyes open for any scheming or trickery.

Coban stepped forward between the two combatants and the crowd fell silent.

"A challenge has been issued. Thomas Kestrel has passed the three Tests. If he wins, he is truly the Highland Lord. If Shagan wins, he earns the right to take the Tests. Are you ready?"

Both Thomas and Shagan nodded.

"Then begin."

Not wasting a second, with a bloodcurdling cry Shagan charged forward, swinging his massive axe down in a savage blow. If it connected, Thomas would have been split in two, but he ducked under it and brought his sword up. Shagan recovered with remarkable speed, slashing at Thomas' throat, but Thomas caught the strike on his claymore and turned it away.

Shagan continued his assault, probing for some weakness, but each time his axe met the steel of Thomas' blade. The speed of Shagan's attack surprised Thomas, but he allowed the larger man to maintain his pace. Thomas used the time to study Shagan's style. The longer Shagan maintained his attack, the more it worked to Thomas' advantage.

Seeing that his assault gained him nothing, Shagan tried a different approach.

"So Green Eyes wants to be the Highland Lord, does he? Our little goblin? The Highland Lord? Now that would be a sight."

The taunt jolted Thomas, and he almost paid for it with his life. Shagan swung high, then turned the blade in mid-air, aiming the slash toward Thomas' chest. Thomas turned his sword just in time to deflect the blow, but it took him longer to regain his concentration. No one had called him goblin for such a long time, it had taken him by surprise. Only the children at the Crag had done so, which meant Shagan had been there as well. That fact sent Thomas' mind down a shadowy path. Something just wasn't right. But what?

"What was it like, boy, being the son of a witch? Did the bitch know what a tiny pup you grew up to be, so unlike your father and grandfather?"

Thomas' eyes smoldered with anger, unable to ignore the jibe. It was time to end this. He had learned Shagan's weaknesses. Now to make use of that knowledge. Thomas sidestepped another slash, then lunged forward, his sword scoring on Shagan's thigh. Though not a serious wound, Shagan screamed more in shock that he had been wounded than in any real pain.

Thomas didn't stop there. His sword became a blur as he attacked, Shagan having a hard time maintaining his defenses. Thomas scored another hit on Shagan's chest, then across his forearm and side. Thomas continued the furious pace of his assault, waiting for the right moment. Then he had it. Seeing the opening he wanted, Thomas brought his sword up for the killing blow.

He was just about to deliver it when the Dark Magic struck him. He was blind! Thomas fell to one knee, not expecting this type of attack. Then he realized it couldn't be Shagan, it had to be someone else. Thomas quickly staggered back, trying to get a feel for his now foreign surroundings, but he stumbled and fell on his back in his haste. The crowd murmured in surprise and concern, thinking just moments before that Thomas was about to defeat the challenger. They had not expected such a reversal.

Sensing that the tide had turned, Shagan laughed as he stood over Thomas.

"A good day to die, don't you think?"

The large Highlander brought his sword down in a vicious blow. Thomas sensed the motion and he quickly extended his senses. He may not be able to see, but he could still defend himself – or at least try to.

Thomas brought his sword up just in time, catching the axe on his blade. Nevertheless, Shagan refused to disengage, pushing with all his might, the muscles bulging in his neck from the effort. Thomas felt the blade of the axe getting closer to his throat, but he wasn't strong enough to throw the axe off his sword. Knowing that if he didn't act quickly, he was going to die, Thomas lashed out with his foot, catching Shagan between the legs.

The blow caught the big Highlander by surprise, and he stumbled back in pain. Thomas immediately pushed himself up from the ground, having gained a brief respite. Shagan couldn't work Dark Magic. Thomas would have known if he could immediately. That left only a few other possibilities, and regardless of what type of creature it was, it had to be close.

Before he could solve the mystery, Shagan was on him once more, having recovered from Thomas' last-ditch defensive tactic. With his vision gone, Thomas had no choice but to focus all his concentration on using all his other senses to fight, which meant he could do nothing with the Talent. If he mistimed its use, he could very well die from Shagan's blade before he found the source of the Dark Magic.

No, he had to try something else. Thomas' movements grew jerky and less certain, sending a rumble of concern through the crowd. Finally, Thomas had an idea. He charged forward, swinging his sword blindly and forcing Shagan to defend himself. He quickly broke off the attack. Thomas used the few seconds to his advantage.

Oso, Thomas called, using his senses to connect to Oso's mind. His friend was clearly taken aback by the communication.

Thomas, how did you do—

That's not important, Oso. I need your help. Something is aiding Shagan. I can't see. Something has used Dark Magic to blind me. You've got to stop—

Thomas was forced to break the communication, Shagan once again taking the offensive. But Oso knew what to do, his face turning an angry red. He should have expected something like this. And judging by Thomas' movements he had to hurry. His friend's life depended on it.

Oso pushed his way through the crowd with Aric and several of the other Highlanders from Raven's Peak following. He explained to them quickly what Thomas had communicated. They all searched the crowd for something out of place, but saw nothing. Then Oso realized that anyone using Dark Magic would clearly stand out, so he led his men past the crowd and toward the tents and pavilions. He knew exactly which one to check first.

Thomas continued to do his best to avoid the blows, darting from side to side and keeping his sword in constant motion, trying to keep Shagan at bay. But eventually Shagan would break through. All Thomas could do now was hope Oso succeeded. Just then Thomas stumbled under another ferocious attack. Thomas slipped to one knee as Shagan's blade finally struck true, slicing across Thomas' left forearm. His hands quickly became wet with blood.

Shagan refused to give him a chance to rise, driving his axe down for the kill. Thomas caught the blow on his blade, but because of his weakened forearm, the grip on his sword slipped and it fell from his hands. Thomas grabbed Shagan's hands, keeping the axe from his head. He tried desperately to dislodge the large Highlander, but he couldn't. Shagan was too strong. With a cold certainty Thomas knew this was the end.

"You're going to die," whispered Shagan, his grey whiskers scratching against Thomas' face. "Ironic, isn't it? In that in a way I killed your father and grandfather, too."

Chapter Forty-One

Vengeance

O so drew his sword, his men following his example, as they approached Shagan's tent. No one was around, as every Highlander now watched the challenge, and clearly from the sounds Oso knew he better hurry. He and his men burst through the tent flap, momentarily blinded by the dark interior. Then Oso saw the movement off to one side.

A Shade!

Screaming in rage, he charged forward. The Shade was so engrossed in his use of the Dark Magic, having to maintain constant control otherwise Thomas would be able to break free of the spell, that the creature didn't realize he was under attack until the last instant. Still, the Shade was fast enough to draw his sword and meet Oso's blow. However, he had not expected the three other blades that followed after, all three sinking deeply into its chest.

The Shade dropped to the floor, a black liquid that could only be its blood flowing out onto the grass. Still, the Shade's milky white eyes held onto life, so Oso brought his sword down with all his might, severing the creature's head from its neck.

A Shade could survive many things, Oso knew, but not that.

CHAPTER FORTY-TWO

STANDING ON HIGH

S hagan's confession unlocked a door in Thomas that he had kept closed for half his life, his rage rushing forth like a torrent. He finally had a target for his hate and anger. And just then, his vision returned. It was as if the spirit of his grandfather smiled down on him, but he knew it was truly Oso. His friend had succeeded.

His growing rage filled Thomas with a new strength, and with Shagan's axe closing in on his throat, in a sudden burst of strength, Thomas threw the larger Highlander off of him. Thomas stood slowly, wiping his bloody hands on his shirt, then taking up the Sword of the Highlands once more with a renewed purpose.

"You must now fight me on your own," said Thomas in a quiet, determined voice that traveled the length of the plateau, Shagan's face turning white with fear. The large Highlander knew in his heart that somehow the Shade had failed. "Now you will pay for what you have done to my family and to my homeland."

Thomas attacked with a savage energy, his sword a whirlwind of motion. His eyes burned a bright green, his face twisted into a vicious snarl. Thomas' attack was too much for Shagan. A crosscut from Thomas knocked the axe from his hands. Though he knew his opponent was now unarmed, there was no mercy for traitors. Thomas brought his sword down in a vicious blow, splitting open Shagan's head, the gore splattering some of the Highlanders in the first few ranks.

A cheer erupted from the Highlanders, but it quickly died. Oso walked through the crowd and into the open space, Aric and the others behind him. In his hand, he carried the head of the Shade. All the Highlanders had seen such a sight before, but none had ever expected to see a Shade here in their most sacred place. Their shock was evident.

Coban stepped forward. "Oso, where did you—"

"Shagan's tent."

He dropped the head on the ground by the dead man's body.

"There's your traitor, Coban," said Thomas, pointing to Shagan. "There's the man who destroyed the Crag."

For a moment Coban just stared, his face twisting with spasms of pain and memory. Then he spit on Shagan's body, his anger having no other outlet. The traitor died too well in his opinion. Then he turned his mind to other things as the Highlanders continued to gaze upon the head of the Shade, the milky white eyes holding them in rapt attention.

The Swordmaster ascended the Pinnacle with Thomas right behind him. The movement broke the spell, yet the Highlanders didn't know whether to cheer Thomas' victory or yell in outrage at the knowledge that a former Marcher and a Highland chief had allied himself with the Shadow Lord's spawn. Coban didn't give them a chance to decide.

"Thomas Kestrel," he pronounced, taking the silver circlet from where he had left it on top of the Pinnacle and placing it on Thomas' head.

"You have passed the Tests and the challenge. More important, you have avenged the destruction of the Crag by finding the traitor among us. I declare you the Highland Lord."

Gasps issued from the crowd and Coban jumped back a step. Standing next to Thomas Kestrel was the spirit of his grandfather, Talyn. The image remained for an instant longer, then disappeared, but the approval in the former Highland Lord's eyes was apparent.

Then the cheers rang out long and hard. Coban having stepped down from the Pinnacle, Thomas stood there on his own taking it all in. The noise lasted for several minutes, and only stopped when Thomas raised his bloody hands for silence. He suddenly realized that he still carried his sword in his hand, the blade still red with Shagan's blood. But he didn't care. He had done it. He had fulfilled his promise to his grandfather and become the Highland Lord. Now the truly difficult part was about to begin. He had to fulfill the promise he had made to his people when he assumed the responsibilities of the Highland Lord while in the Ravine.

"I must be honest with you. I am a Kestrel, true, but my mother wasn't a Highlander. And I have not lived among you for half my life, during a time when you and your families suffered. For that, I am sorry. But that, in part, is why I returned. I could not allow what has happened in my homeland to continue, and I knew that my coming home and serving in the position once held by my grandfather was the only way to do this. I cannot ask you to forgive me for my delay in returning. All I can ask is that you give me a chance to prove my worth."

Thomas ran his eyes across the Highlanders, many obviously having that question of why he waited to return on their minds, but still giving him the benefit of the doubt.

"For almost a decade, the Highlands has been silent, forgotten by the Kingdoms," continued Thomas, speaking from his heart. He had never thought past this moment, so the words flowed from his mouth unbidden.

"The High King's reivers have ravaged our land, stealing our resources and murdering our people. As a result we did something we rarely do – we defended. We did not attack."

"How were we supposed to attack?" someone shouted from the crowd. "We have no defense against the warlocks' Dark Magic?"

Several Highlanders nodded their agreement.

"We fought them as best we could," said another, again earning sounds of agreement from his compatriots. "But we were outnumbered. How are you supposed to fight against so many reivers when you are so few?"

Thomas studied the crowd for a moment, framing his response. These men had fought for ten years, doing the best they could with what they had, but the losing struggle had taken its toll. The spark of hope had returned to their eyes, but they did not truly believe yet

213

that they could defeat the reivers and their warlocks. They did not truly believe in themselves.

"When I was a boy, before I went to sleep my grandfather told me the history of the Highlands and the incredible exploits of the Marchers."

His eyes swept across the crowd, catching as many Highlanders as possible with his gaze.

"He told stories about how one Highland Marcher was the equal of ten soldiers from any other Kingdom. How a Marcher would kneel to no man. How a Marcher would sooner die than accept defeat. Has so much changed in just ten years? Have so many forgotten what it is like to be a Marcher?"

Many of the men looked down at the ground in shame, their embarrassment clear.

"I know you did the best you could, that you fought from a position of weakness. But no longer. The time has come to reclaim what was ours," continued Thomas, his voice low but carrying to everyone's ears. "The time has come to show the High King the price he must pay for what he has done to us."

His words were beginning to sink in, he could see. They were beginning to believe. Now was the time to capture their hearts and souls.

"I have no doubts that if we were to face the reivers in a fair battle, the Highlands would be free once more. But you're right, we did not have a weapon for fighting the warlocks. We have not had one for centuries. Until now."

In a flash of light, the Sword of the Highlands burst into blue flames, as Thomas channeled the Talent into the hardened steel. Gasps of surprise echoed throughout the crowd. Thomas raised the blade above his head so all could see, its brightness illuminating the plateau that was in the process of being covered by the encroaching evening.

"Some called my mother a witch because of her special abilities. But she was not a witch, nor am I. I hold within me the power to defeat the warlocks. Ask Oso and the men of Raven's Peak. They know what I can do. They saw what happened to the Black Hole."

The destruction of the Black Hole was now legendary among the Highlanders, the news of the daring escape traveling to the smallest hamlet of the Highlands. And they had all heard the stories. Yet many had not believed, thinking they were exaggerations, until now.

"Leave the warlocks to me."

And with that Thomas increased the intensity of the flames licking the claymore until they were almost blinding to look at. He saw it in their eyes now. Their spirits and hopes were returning. Now to capture them completely. Gathering the Talent within him, he released a bolt of energy toward the cliffs on the far side of the plateau. The white-hot ball streaked through air and struck with its full force. As the flames died away, shock emanated throughout the crowd. The mark of the Kestrels burned brightly on the cliff face, the flames scoring the stone deeply.

"My friends, let the word go out that the Highland Lord has returned, and with it the strength of the Highlands. Beware the sharp blade of the Marchers, and woe to those who fail to heed us. This is our land, our home, and we will be free once more!"

The Highlanders could contain themselves no longer, captured by the vision of Thomas Kestrel standing atop the Pinnacle, the Sword of the Highlands burning brightly in his hand. And that fire soon matched the one now burning in their hearts – their desire for freedom.

From the back of the crowd a set of bagpipes began to play, and then another, and another, until the night was filled with the haunting tones that drifted to every corner of the Highlands. It was a sound most had not heard since the time of Talyn Kestrel. It was a call to arms. The Highlands prepared for war.

CHAPTER FORTY-THREE

CONFIRMATION

Rynlin Keldragan rose from where he had been studying several distinct tracks in the blackened ash that covered the Charnel Mountains. Ogren. A lot of them, by the look of things. But that didn't concern him at the moment. He turned toward the west, staring in that direction for several minutes. Then a smile creased his hard visage.

Sensing his grandson through his necklace, he knew that Thomas had succeeded. His grandson was the Highland Lord. His pride almost burst from him, but his mind quickly moved on to the next step in what he saw to be a far more important process.

Thomas was one step closer to becoming the Defender of the Light. The lines of the prophecy that he knew so well ran through his mind.

> *When a child of life and death*
> *Stands on high*
> *Drawn by faith*
> *He shall hold the key to victory in his hand.*
>
> *Swords of fire echo in the burned rock*

Balancing the future on their blades.

Light dances with dark
Green fire burns in the night
Hopes and dreams follow the wind
To fall in black or white.

Stands on high. A common name for when some-one becomes a Highland Lord, for that person is standing on the Pinnacle. It simply confirmed when Thomas became a Sylvan Warrior, when a similar reference was made. Though the struggle to free the Highlands was important, the true battle for freedom, for the light, was coming.

He was certain of that. He just didn't know when.

If you really enjoyed this story, I need you to do me a HUGE favor — please write a review. It helps the book and me. I really appreciate the feedback. Consider a review on Amazon or BookBub at https://www.bookbub.com/profile/peter-wacht.

Follow me on my website at www.kestrelmg.com to keep an eye out for the next book in the series … or perhaps even a new story.

Made in the USA
Monee, IL
12 June 2022